'I'll Touch You When I Want to, Keely,'

he said. 'You didn't mind so much last night.'

She stopped struggling—it was useless, anyway—and looked up into his dark face. 'Last night I was . . . affected by the dancing. This morning I'm of sound mind, and I *loathe* you, Jordan!'

'You kissed me back—'

'In that mood, I'd have kissed any man back!'

'You wanted *me*. You couldn't hide it.'

She made one futile attempt to escape, and then his merciless kiss bent her head back and his mouth possessed hers.

LAUREY BRIGHT
discovered the magic of reading early in life, and hopes that her books will bring the same magic to others. Although her interests are varied—including history and ecology—she first began writing love stories at sixteen, and has never wanted to be anything but a writer.

Dear Reader:

Silhouette Romances is an exciting new publishing venture. We will be presenting the very finest writers of contemporary romantic fiction as well as outstanding new talent in this field. It is our hope that our stories, our heroes and our heroines will give you, the reader, all you want from romantic fiction.

Also, *you* play an important part in our future plans for Silhouette Romances. We welcome any suggestions or comments on our books and I invite you to write to us at the address below.

So, enjoy this book and all the wonderful romances from Silhouette. They're for *you!*

Karen Solem
Editor-in-Chief
Silhouette Books
P. O. Box 769
New York, N.Y. 10019

LAUREY BRIGHT
Tears of Morning

Silhouette Romance

Published by Silhouette Books New York

America's Publisher of Contemporary Romance

SILHOUETTE BOOKS, a Simon & Schuster Division of
GULF & WESTERN CORPORATION
1230 Avenue of the Americas, New York, N.Y. 10020

ISBN: 0-671-57107-9

First Silhouette Books printing October, 1981

10 9 8 7 6 5 4 3 2 1

Tears of
Morning

Chapter One

The heat in Suva was intense, like a warm, damp blanket and almost as suffocating at times. Keely, her camera at the ready, tried to emulate the slow movements of the local population. The Fijians walked at a leisurely pace, their splendid physiques investing them with an impressive stateliness as they made their way among the cosmopolitan crowds that thronged the noisy marketplace. The graceful Indian women in their flowing saris looked cool and dainty, browsing among the tables piled high with a fantastic variety of wares, from locally grown fruits and Fijian handcrafted goods to lengths of bright cotton materials and imported toiletries and perfumes. A tall, bearded Sikh, his turban tootpaste-white, towered for a few moments above a party of smiling Japanese seamen as he passed them, and a group of French sailors interestedly eyed a couple of strikingly lovely Polynesian girls in smart, fashionable dresses and high-heeled sandals. One had tucked a scarlet hibiscus blossom into her long, gleaming black hair, the bright petals just touching her smooth olive-skinned cheek, and the other had looped her tresses into an intricate mass of plaits and coils set off by a tortoise-shell comb.

Keely quickly raised her camera and got a shot of the girls with the sailors in the background, admiration on their faces. One of the girls looked at her as they passed and smiled rather shyly. She didn't seem to mind about the photograph. The tourist trade was heavy in Suva, and there were parties of Australians, Americans and even Germans, happily snapping pictures and hunting for bargains in the cheerful, colourful jumble of the market.

A trio of Samoan women sat on a woven mat, their quick fingers weaving palm-leaf baskets with deceptive ease as they laughed and gossiped, and a Chinese vendor offered her a very special price on a transistor radio, which she refused. Wending her way among the stalls, appreciating the shade intermittently provided by a haphazard series of makeshift awnings made from faded canvas, or bright sailcloth, or even flower-printed lengths of cotton, she looked at her watch, but there was still a half hour to fill before her appointment.

When at last she decided it was time to leave the market and found herself a taxi, she was conscious of a fluttering in her stomach and a tiny, throbbing pain at her temple that was due to nothing but nerves.

She took a compact from her bag and smoothed lipstick over her mouth, annoyed to find that her hand was shaking. The tan she had acquired in the last few weeks suited her, and although her nose felt shiny in the heat, it didn't look it. Her green eyes looked slightly apprehensive, but her appearance was one of confidence. Her honey-coloured hair was neatly swept back into a knot, and her dress was still uncrushed, the satin finish on the cotton giving a sophisiticated look to the design of green leaves on a silver-grey background, the trim belted style emphasising a slim waist, high breasts and nicely rounded hips.

The taxi racketed through the traffic, stopping only for the white-gloved, imperiously uplifted hand of a huge black policeman wearing a red jacket and white lava-lava, its distinctive edge cut into a series of points below the knee.

Arriving at a waterfront building, she was ushered immediately into Michael Ward's office. He rose from behind the desk and gave her a dazzling smile, saying, 'I'm Michael Ward. How can I help you, Miss Alexander?'

He was tanned to a coppery hue and extremely good-looking, making her blink for a moment in sheer admiration as she sat down and handed him the letter in which her publisher explained, to whom it might concern, that she was commissioned to write a book on North Americans who had their own Pacific hideaways.

Michael Ward read it, laughed and tossed the letter carelessly back across the desk to her. 'You mean you're after the white man's dream?' he grinned.

Keely hesitated, then smiled tentatively and said, 'Yes. I'm afraid that *is* what I mean. People in the northern hemisphere have always been fascinated by the Pacific, right back to Gauguin and Robert Louis Stevenson. They still are—'

'And you want to write a book about the ones who have actually done something about it? The film stars who have bought themselves a Pacific island?' He seemed to be enjoying the idea, rocking his chair back on its rear legs as he pushed his hands into his pockets, his nearly black eyes dancing. 'So you've come to a shipping agent—but I'm afraid we don't provide service to any film stars. They can afford to have their supplies dropped by helicopter. And they like their privacy.'

'You provide service to Salutu.'

For a moment he went on smiling at her. Then the chair legs thumped back on the floor and the humour in his eyes turned to blank surprise.

'What do you know about Salutu?' he demanded.

Her hands tightened on the letter she had just

retrieved from the desk. 'There's a Canadian there,' she said. She moistened her lips with her tongue and added, 'His name is Jordan Lang. I want to interview him.'

Michael Ward looked at her with regret. 'You've picked the wrong man,' he said. 'Find a film star. They *like* publicity.'

'I found one,' she said, smiling. 'And I've interviewed him—but it wasn't easy. I had to promise not to say just where his island is. He wasn't all that keen on the publicity, in fact. Now I'm after a different angle.'

'Jordan Lang's angle? I'm afraid you're wasting your time, Miss Alexander.'

'You have a supply boat going there soon, haven't you?'

'In a few days, yes. But—'

'Then I'd like to book a berth to Salutu.'

'The *Alena* is a cargo boat,' he said promptly.

Keely looked at him silently for a moment or two, her head slightly tipped to one side, her mouth curved in a sceptical smile. Gently, almost teasing, she said, 'Now, Mr. Ward, she does have passenger accommodation.'

'She's not a tourist ship,' he said. 'We pick up phosphate from there, you know.'

She hadn't known, but she had learned not to betray surprise at new facts. 'I'm not a tourist,' she said. 'I'm a working journalist. I'm not fussy about the accommodation, as long as I get there.'

'It's a slow trip. There are other islands to be called at on the way.'

'How slow?'

'Three days.'

'Well, it's the only way, isn't it? Yours is the only ship that calls at Salutu, and I've been told I can't get there by plane.'

'There's no place for one to land,' he confirmed, frowning. 'Look, I'm sure you'll be wasting your time.

Jordan won't agree to an interview, I can tell you that now.'

'Jordan? Is Mr. Lang a personal friend of yours, Mr. Ward?'

'I know him. And I know he won't want to be in your book.'

Softly, she said, 'I just want the chance to try to persuade him, Mr. Ward, that's all. Please—book me a place on your ship.'

'Jordan will kill me!' the man groaned.

Keely laughed. 'Oh, surely not! Anyway, *you* won't be there—*I* will! If you like, I won't tell him that you know why I want to see him.'

He took some persuading, but eventually he capitulated, and she could not be unaware that it was at least partly because he found her attractive. He arranged her ticket, then asked if he could take her out to dinner. Keely accepted, but any hope that she might have been able to pump him about Jordan Lang was squashed by his laughing refusal to talk about another man while in the company of a pretty girl.

She rebuffed his more obvious advances, sure that with his looks there were plenty of other girls ready to succumb to his undoubted charm, and she was back in her hotel room before midnight.

The *Alena* was a steamship, squat and workmanlike, and the paint was peeling off her metal sides. She had none of the grace of the shabby but still romantic-looking sailing scows that plied round some of the islands. The few other passengers were Fijians returning to villages on scattered atolls, laden with pieces of cloth and manufactured goods from Suva. Keely spent her days talking to and photographing them, and her two evenings ashore with the captain, being introduced to Fijian customs and the numbing but strangely refreshing taste of *yaqona,* the muddy-looking ceremonial drink offered with gravity by their hosts.

Sven, the captain, was a big, blond Swede, and she

never discovered his last name. When she told him why she was going to Salutu, he roared with laughter. 'An interview with Jordan?' he said incredulously. 'Does he expect you?'

'No,' she said.

'I'm looking forward to seeing his face!' Sven grinned. 'You had better make sure I'm there to hold your hand when you tell him what you want. Didn't Mike warn you?'

'He said he thought I was wasting my time.'

'But you still came?'

'I'm a very persistent person.'

'A reporter.' He eyed her thoughtfully.

'A photojournalist,' Keely corrected firmly.

'Somehow I don't think Jordan will appreciate the difference.'

Keely felt herself tensing, and tried to relax and speak casually. 'Doesn't he like journalists?' she asked.

'A reporter from Suva came out and tried to interview him once. The poor guy ended up in the lagoon.'

Keely frowned. 'What do you mean?'

'I mean that Jordan got fed up with being questioned when he didn't want to talk, and he threw the reporter into the sea and advised him to swim back to the ship.'

Keely was silent for a moment. Then, 'He sounds a perfectly charming man,' she said. 'Is he always so violent?'

'Oh, I guess you'll be safe enough,' Sven said. 'Even Jordan Lang wouldn't do a thing like that to you. You're much too pretty. Although . . .' he added, 'could be you'd look just as pretty after a ducking.' His glance slid over the clinging tee-shirt she wore with her denim shorts, and she couldn't help smiling a little because he was so blatant.

It was all on the surface and nothing meant by it, though Sven liked her and thought she was pretty. She wasn't averse to admiration, no woman could be, but she didn't intend to let it go any further than that. Her mind was already winging ahead to the island with the romantic, musical name, her heart pounding unevenly as she wondered what Jordan Lang's reaction to her invasion of his Pacific retreat would be. Jordan Lang. Memory stirred, briefly and painfully, before she resolutely brought her mind back to the present.

When Salutu rose from the haze on the horizon in the late afternoon of the third day, she was on deck in jeans and a windbreaker, a nippy sea breeze blowing her hair across her cheeks. When the ship dropped anchor on the green satin sea outside the reef enclosing the island, she went below to change into a tan skirt and brief flowered top, then combed her hair and tied it with a bright scarf before making the journey to shore in a canoe manned by tall, dark-skinned paddlers, stroking with beautiful, economical movements for the beach.

She saw the water breaking on the reef, and they seemed to skim over the coral, the sea only fractionally deep enough to cover the sharp coral spikes showing whitely through the waves; and then they were in the clear blue water of the lagoon itself, glassy and transparent, tiny fish darting sinuously away from the prow and the shallows littered with speckled, twisted and patterned shells.

Keely kept her eyes on the water until one of the paddlers leaped over the side, followed by another, and the canoe ran onto the sand, helped by their hefty pushes. She had a glimpse of many people standing about and of children running to meet the passengers. Sven stood up and picked up the canvas bag into which she had stowed her camera, tape recorder and spare films and tapes, slung it over his own shoulder, then stepped into the shallow water to scoop her up in his arms and carry her onto the dry powdery white sand.

'It wasn't so bad, was it?' he murmured in her ear, his breath tickling her skin.

She realised that he had noticed her nervousness and thought she was afraid of the journey from ship to shore by outrigger canoe.

As he set her on her feet she saw a figure separate itself from the others in the crowd. Her eyes blurred with fright and something very close to tears as she took in brown feet in rope-soled sandals, faded khaki trousers covering long legs with powerful thighs revealed by the thin, much-washed material; a white cotton shirt with rolled sleeves was open over a broad, tanned chest with a smattering of dark hair curling over it. Her eyes paused at the unexpected sharp, curved shark tooth hung on a leather thong about the strong neck, and she noticed that the sinews of that neck were rather prominent, the jutting jaw above tight and uncompromising. Her heart plunged as she skimmed past a taut, sculpted mouth, a straight, rather forbidding nose, high cheekbones with an Indian look, accentuated by coal-dark hair that had been allowed to grow beyond collar-length, though its crisp, glossy waves had been pushed back from a broad, black-browed forehead. He had changed very little, but there was a hardness in him that made some indefinable difference to his expression.

She met his eyes at last because she could no longer avoid them and drew in a sharp, inaudible breath. His eyes, which had once been lit with passion and tenderness, were the deep metallic grey of the sea on a sullen, stormy day. They looked at her now with a fierce, intense concentration. At first that was all she could read in them. This was a new Jordan, not the man she had once known intimately but a stranger to be treated with caution. She met his inimical stare warily.

Sven said, 'This is Miss Keely Alexander, Jordan. She's writing a book about Pacific hermits like you, my friend. She wants you to give her an interview.'

Keely couldn't say anything, standing on the white coral sand with the sun beating down, her wide green eyes fixed on Jordan Lang's dark, chiselled face. At first she thought he hadn't heard; there was no change of expression in the cloud-dark eyes. Then his mouth moved a little, twisted at the corner oddly, and his eyes blazed suddenly into a strange mixture of incredulity and sheer cold fury.

Chapter Two

Jordan Lang still hadn't taken his eyes off her. When he spoke his voice was low, but so harsh that she inwardly flinched. 'I don't give interviews,' he said.

Then he turned away, shook hands with Sven and exchanged a few words with one of the islanders standing nearby.

For a moment or two Keely sagged in sheer relief that the meeting, at least, was over. She looked about her and saw a narrow, white beach, dark palms pressing against its edge, rising ground behind and, in the distance, a symmetrical volcanic cone covered thickly by a green jungle of tropical trees.

She became aware of whispering voices near at hand and turned to find herself being surveyed by a dozen or more pairs of curious brown eyes. The men had begun moving away along the beach, but the women and children seemed anxious to make her acquaintance. They were smiling, and one plump woman came forward with a hand outstretched and said, 'My name is Eta Bali. Welcome.'

From the corner of her eye Keely was aware of grey eyes swivelling to watch as she took the brown hand in hers and said clearly, 'I'm Keely Alexander. Thank you for your welcome.'

She was introduced to all of them then, her head reeling with the names but her stumbling tongue trying to pronounce them, making the children laugh and their mothers hide their smiles politely behind raised hands.

Sven called to her and she turned, aware that Jordan Lang was standing impatiently by with thumbs hooked into the belt of his faded trousers while Sven came across the sand to touch her arm and say, 'We're going up to Jordan's house for a drink.'

Suddenly angry at the other man's lack of manners, she said clearly, so that he could not help but hear her, 'Am I invited?'

Jordan Lang's expression didn't change, but Sven looked faintly embarrassed and said, 'Of course. Come on.'

She said goodbye to the islanders, and by the time she had walked with Sven across the hot sand into the shade of the palms, their host was striding ahead, up a steep path bordered by breadfruit and palm trees and hibiscus with lazy bees hovering about their quivering stamens. He didn't even look to see if they were coming.

When the house came into view, Keely stopped suddenly in sheer surprise, and Sven grinned down at her and said, 'Quite something, isn't it?'

'That's an understatement!' she retorted. 'It's—it's about the most wildly improbable thing I've ever seen in my life!'

Someone, she thought, must have had delusions of grandeur. It was a southern mansion set down in the middle of the Pacific. White, gracious, pillared and porticoed and pretentious, two storeys of exotic elegance and sprawling space that must have looked impossibly civilised on this island wilderness when it

was built—when? About the turn of the century, at a
guess. But over the years it had melded into its tropical
setting, the lantana and hibiscus and banana trees
softening the starkness of the white stone, the patina of
time smoothing the incongruity as the house settled
into its strange surroundings.

Keely walked on, at Sven's urging, with the sudden
conviction that this was all some sort of dream. The
beautiful white house, the pink and scarlet trumpets of
hibiscus that nodded against the pillars, the scent of
sandalwood and ginger and jasmine that lay heavy and
sweet on the air seemed strangely unreal. But as they
approached the broad flight of shallow steps that led to
a great carved door standing open, her eyes met the
hard gaze of the man who had stopped there to wait for
them—and he was real, all right. There was nothing
dreamlike about the lean strength of his body, the
muscles that showed under the rolled sleeves of his
shirt, the faint dew of sweat she could see on his
half-bared chest as she drew near.

He turned abruptly and led them into the house.
Keely had an impression of a cool, dark, high-ceilinged
interior and wide stairs curving up one side of the
entrance hall. With the sun's dazzle still in her eyes, she
saw only the vague outline of a woman standing by the
stair rail and heard the murmur of her voice before she
disappeared into the shadows beyond the stairs.

'In here,' Jordan Lang said, and they went into a
room at the front of the house. It was a long room with
one wall of shuttered windows, which he opened,
giving them a view through moving trees of the peaceful sea, shading from green near the island to a deeper
green streaked with indigo to a band of hazy purple on
the distant horizon.

There were comfortable cane loungers and cushioned chairs, a faded oriental carpet of age-blurred
beauty and small, intricately carved tables inlaid with
mother-of-pearl. Overhead a huge electric fan stirred
the air.

'Sit down.' The invitation was flung over his shoulder as he pushed at a recalcitrant shutter, and Sven saw Keely seated before he took a chair himself.

Sven had chosen for them two of four chairs that were grouped around one of the low carved tables. They sat facing the sea, and she resolutely kept her eyes on the view as their host took a seat facing them. A short silence fell, and then Jordan looked up as a woman appeared in the doorway with a tray in her hands.

She came into the room and he went to meet her, taking the tray from her to set it down on the table. Keely turned to look at her and caught her breath. The woman was quite beautiful, her face exquisitely lovely, perfectly oval and with a warm golden bloom on the skin. Long black hair was drawn back at the temples and caught with a tortoise-shell comb with one perfect orange-gold hibiscus bloom tucked into it, then allowed to fall in shining tresses to her waist. Her long skirt was made of a single length of brightly coloured cotton, tied at one side of her trim waist and showing glimpses of a smooth golden leg as she moved, and a white embroidered blouse was drawn tightly across a pretty bosom and tied at the front.

Sven rose from his chair and said, 'Hello, Tila. You get more beautiful each time I see you.'

The girl flashed him a smile and turned her face aside a little as though she was shy. But she gave him her hand and said 'Hello, Sven. Was the trip good?'

'Very good—I had a lovely companion this time.'

She gave a soft laugh and cast a curious glance at Keely, saying, 'Ah— your *kai valagi* friend!'

Sven performed the introduction, and Tila smiled warmly. Then the island girl turned to the other man and said, 'Is there anything else you want, Jordan?'

He smiled at her, the first smile Keely had seen him give anyone since their arrival, and said easily, 'I don't think so, Tila. This looks fine. Thank you.'

Sven said, 'Aren't you going to join us?'

'I have work to do,' Tila told him calmly. 'Besides, if I eat too much I will get fat—then I will not be so beautiful to you, eh, Sven?'

He grinned and said, 'You'd be fat and beautiful—anyway, why should you worry? You've got your man, as you're always telling me.'

'And you've got a girl in every port,' she retorted. But she was laughing at him over her shoulder as she left the room and Sven resumed his seat.

Jordan was pouring iced lime juice from a tall glass jug on the tray before him. His face looked grim and tight-jawed. Without looking at Keely, he said, 'Would you like a dash of gin in yours, Miss Alexander?'

She said, 'Thank you, Mr. Jordan.' She could do with something bracing at the moment.

His eyes flicked up to her face, and she fancied that he hadn't liked her formal tone. Well, he had started it, with that deliberate *Miss Alexander*. His glance was immediately withdrawn, and she realised that he didn't want to look at her. But he kept looking all the same, his eyes unwillingly dragged in her direction time and again as they sipped their drinks and bit into the small, freshly baked coconut cakes that Tila had made. He wanted to ignore her, but he couldn't. Slowly, the tight knot of tension in her stomach began to unwind. The first hurdle was over. He hadn't yet threatened to throw her into the lagoon. And he couldn't keep his eyes off her. She allowed herself a tiny, perhaps slightly complacent smile, and when the grey eyes swerved again, reluctantly, to her face, she let the smile tilt her mouth a little at the corners and held his gaze for a long moment with her clear green one.

His eyes narrowed before he wrenched them away from hers to concentrate on what Sven was saying to him. Keely felt a little shaken, because what she had read in them that time was hostility—unmistakable and dangerous.

Jordan suddenly put down his glass and said, 'Well,

we'd better start loading.' He stood up, and Sven finished the inch of lime juice in his glass and followed suit.

'Can I come and watch?' Keely asked, standing up, too, and looking directly at Jordan Lang.

'You'll see it all from the ship,' he said indifferently.

Keely flushed a little with anger, and Sven looked at her apologetically.

They went down to the beach, and Keely realised that the islanders had been busy. A haphazard pile of boxes and sacks was on the beach, and a laden canoe was coming in to the shore as they watched, bringing the last of the supplies.

Back on board, the anchor was lifted and they cruised slowly part of the way around the island. Keely bit back a shocked exclamation as she saw where they were to stop this time.

The reef was still there, cutting them off from the lagoon, but there was an appreciable, though narrow, gap here. The island above the narrow strip of sand had been torn up, ravaged—*desecrated* was the word that came into her mind as she took in the huge scars of excavation, the ugly tin buildings scattered about the rocky ground that was stripped of all vegetation and the gaunt lines of cranes towering above the grey-white surface. There were squat yellow bulldozers along the outer rim of the excavation, and long storage sheds replaced the tall palms to one side of the bay.

A motorised barge left the beach and came through the gap in the reef, and one of the ship's gantries lowered some boxes and sacking-wrapped bundles onto it for transport to shore. Jordan, who had disappeared with Sven as soon as they came on board, reappeared and swung himself down over the side and onto the barge. Later, from her position on deck, she caught glimpses of him among the men busy on shore, helping as the barges were loaded with sacks of phosphate.

The ship's crew had been augmented by a score of smiling, singing islanders who helped to stack the phosphate in the hold, their every movement like a carefully choreographed ballet as they took a bag from the stacks being lowered by the gantry, shifted it onto their shoulders and piled it neatly into place with the others. She took the camera out of the bag, which Sven had carried all the way to Jordan Lang's house and back again without her having had a chance to use it, and began photographing the controlled, efficient operations that were taking place.

Night fell suddenly, like a curtain drawn across the sky.

The islanders left the ship and Jordan came out on the last barge, calling up to Sven. Keely had moved away from the railing when she saw him coming, and Sven leaned over the rail of the ship to talk to him, then turned to her and said, 'Would you like to spend the night ashore?'

'Where?' she asked, and he grinned.

'Jordan's place,' he said.

'Are you going?'

'Sure. The invitation is for both of us.' he told her.

'All right,' she said, her throat tight. 'How do we get there?'

They went on the barge first, and then she sat between the two men on the dusty leather seat of a Landrover and was driven over a rough road. The headlights picked out shiny dark leaves brushing the bonnet, and startled birds shrieked an occasional protest as they passed. Once something like a huge spider scuttled out of their way, and Keely tensed and opened her mouth, then bit her lip hard on the sound she was determined not to make. Jordan must have felt something, even though she had done her best to stop her thigh from touching his, to keep her body rigidly unaware of the warmth and strength of his beside her. He glanced at her pale profile in the darkness and said laconically, 'A land crab. Seen one before?'

She hadn't, and she didn't much want to see one again. She just shook her head silently, and he turned his attention back to the narrow road.

In a surprisingly short time they drew up before the big house, and she got out of the Landrover and took her bag as Sven handed it to her and turned to get his own. Jordan came around the vehicle and took it from her, ignoring her slight protest, and pushed open the big door to let them into the house.

Tila was coming down the stairs, looking infinitely graceful in her long skirt, her bare feet making no sound on the dark polished wood.

They all watched her coming down, and she looked at Jordan and smiled and lifted her eyebrows, as though silently asking a question. Jordan turned to Keely and Sven and said harshly, 'I asked Tila to get two bedrooms ready—is that right?'

As the implication hit her, Keely turned to him with fire in her furious green eyes, finding his grey ones resting with a kind of merciless concentration on her face.

Sven laughed and said, 'That's for Keely to say.'

Keely was so angry she couldn't speak for a moment.

Jordan said with exaggerated patience, 'Well—*Miss* Alexander?'

'Of course it's right!' she said loudly, at last. 'What did you *think?*'

He shrugged, his eyes mocking. 'Do you care what I think, Miss Alexander?'

She wanted to hit him, and she saw that he knew it and it didn't bother him. She said, 'I couldn't care less what you think, Mr. Lang.'

'That's what I thought,' he said softly.

Sven laughed rather nervously, and Tila said quietly, 'We didn't mean to offend you, *marama*. I thought it was best to ask . . .'

'I'm not offended,' Keely said stiffly.

'You'd better show them the rooms, Tila,' Jordan

said curtly. He made to turn away, then looked at Tila again and gave her a rueful smile. 'Please,' he added.

Keely's room was large and airy, sparsely furnished, but with a brass bed that made her exclaim in admiration. There was also a mosquito net that smelled faintly of age and damp, and Tila said, 'I thought you might need a net. I found it in a cupboard.' She twitched frowningly at the folds, and Keely said, 'Does everyone on the island speak such good English?'

'Not everyone, though most of the people speak it a little. I went to school in Australia for three years. If there is anything you need, tell me—the bathroom is just across the passageway. And there are towels and soap here.' She indicated the old-fashioned dressing table near the door.

Keely couldn't think of anything more she might need, and Tila left her, saying that their meal would be ready in about an hour.

She felt hot and sticky. She took a cotton terry robe from her bag, picked up the towels and soap and her toothbrush and went into the bathroom. It was rather impressive. The bath was nearly three feet deep, the shower cubicle big enough for two and the whole room lined with white tiles that had web-fine cracks of age in them. She had a brief, lukewarm shower, not using too much water because she didn't know how the supply was brought to the house and knew that in such places water was sometimes a scarce commodity.

She was crossing the passageway to her room, her hair in damp tendrils on the shoulders of the terry cloth wrap and her clothes over her arm, when Sven came out of his room. She smiled at him and continued to her own room, and she had just closed the door and laid her clothes on the white cotton bedspread when he knocked and softly called her name.

Keely tightened the belt of her robe and opened the door to find him standing very close, so that she automatically stepped back. He took one step into the

room and said, 'Keely . . . I wanted to apologise. You
were embarrassed, weren't you?'

'It wasn't your fault,' she said. 'Don't worry about
it.'

'I joked about it, though. I didn't think you would
mind. Women . . . ' he said, his eyes puzzled, a little
smile on his lips.

'Men!' she shot at him, caustically, and he laughed.

Keely laughed, too, though, having met Jordan
again, she meant the comment more seriously than
Sven might think, and put a hand on his chest to push
him into the passageway. 'Go on,' she said with a smile.
'You're forgiven!'

He moved, but not much. His head leaning consider-
ingly to one side and his eyes teasing, he said, 'You
wouldn't like to change your mind? I wouldn't mind
sharing a room with you.'

'Go on!' Keely said. 'Tila was right about you!'

'All right,' he said agreeably, but he caught her
hands and held them while he bent briefly and kissed
her on the mouth.

Then he backed away, laughing as he released her,
and cannoned into Jordan, who had come up the stairs
while they were absorbed in their laughing, teasing
conversation.

Keely took one fleeting glance at the icy look on
Jordan's face and hastily closed her door on both men.

She smoothed scented talcum powder over her body,
used light makeup on her eyes and lips and put on a
crush-proof synthetic dress in dark greens and blues
splashed with orange flowers resembling tiger lilies. It
was cut on very simple lines, the bodice cleverly shaped
so that she needed no bra, the material clinging softly
to her waist and hips and flaring to her feet. The
neckline dipped into a vee-front, and a low back
showed off her golden tan. She knew she looked good
in it, and tonight she needed the confidence that came
from that knowledge.

It was a go-anywhere dress that she had found very useful; it could look casual with sandals and a shell necklace, or elegant with sparkling earrings and a matching bracelet. She decided on the shell necklace, a long string that almost reached her waist. She brushed her hair and let it fall about her shoulders. There was a definite bright blond streak in the front, she noticed, that she had acquired in the last few weeks. The fierce sun of the islands had bleached it.

The two men were at the bottom of the stairs when she went down, and Sven watched her appreciatively as she descended. Jordan had cast one enigmatic glance at her and then fixed his gaze on something to the left of Sven's shoulder. But she saw his hand resting on the polished stair rail and noticed that his knuckles were white.

It gave her added confidence, and she was able to smile at them both as she joined them and say steadily, 'Have I kept you waiting? I'm sorry.'

Sven gallantly took her hand in his and kissed her fingers. 'You are worth waiting for,' he assured her, his eyes sending mischievous messages. Jordan said nothing and led them into the room that they had been in before.

The shutters were closed now, and electric bulbs glowed from a glass chandelier in the ceiling. At one end of the room a round table had been set with three places on a snowy white cloth with a centrepiece of gardenias and green fern.

Jordan poured them all sherry and handed two glasses to Sven, who passed one to Keely. She took it, returned his silent toast and said to Jordan, 'This is a very civilised home for a hermit, Mr. Lang.'

'I don't call myself a hermit,' he answered. 'That was Sven's term.'

'Well, you certainly have all the modern conveniences,' she said. 'How old is the house?'

'It was built at the turn of the century.'

She waited to see if he would tell her more, but he didn't. 'Where does your electricity come from?' she asked, looking at the chandelier.

'A generator at the back of the house.'

'And your water?'

He sipped his sherry and said in bored tones, 'There's a spring not far from the house. The water has been piped from there ever since the place was built.'

'I've been wondering who did build it,' she said. 'And why.'

'Have you?' His tone was short, and his eyes looked derisive.

Keely drew in a sharp breath as Sven shot Jordan a puzzled look.

Then Tila came into the room, wheeling a tea trolley laden with dishes, and Jordan put down his glass and said, 'Shall we eat?'

The meal was delicious . . . enormous prawns in coconut cream, curried chicken with fluffy rice, taro sliced with green vegetables and cooked in a spicy sauce, roasted pork and sweet potato and a dessert of fresh fruit salad. Tila served them, disappearing between courses to appear with some new delicacy a little later. When she brought in coffee and laid the tray on the low table between the chairs that they had used earlier, Sven said, 'That was magnificent, Tila,' and Jordan asked her to have coffee with them. She shook her head, said something in her own language and went out with the remainder of the dishes.

Keely said tentatively, 'Perhaps I could help with the washing up . . . ?'

Jordan looked over at her and said, 'No. Tila doesn't allow guests in the kitchen. You can pour the coffee if you like.'

She sat in one of the cane chairs and poured coffee for three. She filled Jordan's cup and pushed it over to him, and he leaned over and spooned sugar into the black brew as she poured for Sven, who lay back and

gave a deep sigh of content as he placed a hand on his
stomach and said, 'You lucky man, Jordan. That girl is
one terrific cook.'

'I know,' Jordan said with a faint smile, his eyes on
the cup in his hand.

Keely's nerves tautened. Something about Tila bothered her. She was obviously Jordan's housekeeper.
And she was obviously also something more than a
housekeeper. She served Jordan and his guests, but she
didn't act like a servant and neither Jordan nor Sven
treated her like one. If Keely had not been here, she
was sure that Tila would have had a drink with the men
this afternoon and perhaps had coffee with them this
evening.

What other intimacies did Tila share with her em-
ployer when there was no *kai valagi* woman around to
be shocked by them? Keely felt sick at the thought.

It was stupid to be so shocked, of course. The film
star she had visited on his island had been sharing it
with a curvaceous starlet at the time. She had interviewed another island owner who made no secret of his
virtual harem of buxom island beauties, and he had
made it rather clear that he would not have minded
adding Keely to their number. It was part of the lure of
the islands, the white man's dream that Michael Ward
had laughed about; the fantasy life must include a
lovely maiden or two who would share the Pacific
paradise. Of course Jordan wouldn't be any different.
She should have expected this.

Her hand shook as she lifted her cup and gulped
down a mouthful of hot coffee, burning her tongue and
bringing tears to her eyes. She carefully drank more of
the coffee and put the cup back in the saucer with a
small clatter, then placed them on the table. They were
English bone china, she realised, as she sat back and
found Jordan's eyes on her. She said the first thing that
came into her head. 'Where did your nice china come
from?'

For a moment he looked blank, as though the

question had disconcerted him. Then he said, "It was in the house when I came.'

'It's lovely,' she said. 'Is the furniture original? From when the house was built, I mean?'

'I wouldn't know.'

Sven laughed. 'Why don't you just say, "No comment," Jordan?'

Jordan looked at him, then turned to Keely. 'Am I being interviewed?' he said.

'No. I was just interested.'

'But she would like an interview,' Sven said. 'Why don't you talk to her, Jordan?'

'She doesn't want an interview,' Jordan said flatly.

Keely felt her teeth go tight, and her fingers clenched in her lap. Sven looked incredulous, then he laughed in a puzzled way. 'Of course she does!' he said. 'She came all this way on the *Alena* to talk to you, to do a story on you.'

'Is that what she told you?' Jordan said derisively. 'Why don't you tell Sven the truth, *Miss* Alexander?'

She hated the way he said *Miss Alexander*, the mockery in his eyes, his voice. She looked straight back at him, hatred and contempt in her eyes, making his suddenly narrow and glitter unpleasantly. She said, 'It *is* the truth. I'm a professional journalist and I have a commission for a book. I have a list of people to interview, and you're on it. It's a job, Mr. Lang, a job I intend to do to the best of my ability.'

She could see he didn't believe a word of it, and her temper simmered dangerously. He looked her over with a detached thoroughness that brought her almost to boiling point, and then he said, 'You don't look to me like a professional journalist.'

'Your type of man,' she said bitingly, 'doesn't believe that any woman is capable of doing a job efficiently and still looking like a woman. What would you expect a journalist to wear in the tropics? Tweeds?'

He said, 'I wasn't talking about clothes.'

'I don't think you *know* what you're talking about!'

she said. 'If you'll excuse me for a few minutes, I would like to fetch something to show you.'

She didn't wait for his nod but swept out of the room and up the stairs to the room she had been given. Opening up her overnight bag, she took out the slim vinyl briefcase she had tossed in at the last moment. It contained the letter she had shown to Michael Ward, a folder into which were clipped six published magazine articles with her byline on them and a proof copy of her first book.

She rummaged in the canvas holdall as well and found two ring-bound notebooks, one used and one fresh, and her tape recorder. Burdened with all these, she returned to the lounge. On the stairs she met Tila, who smiled at her and said, 'Do you have all you need for the night, *marama?* I am going to bed now.'

'Yes, thank you,' Keely said tightly. 'Good night.'

She didn't turn to see which room Tila went into. It wouldn't have told her a thing, anyway, since she didn't know where Jordan slept.

When she entered the room, Sven was looking slightly amused and Jordan wore a mask of boredom. She knew it was a mask, and she was determined to force him to let it slip.

She didn't entirely succeed. She thought it shook him when she presented all the evidence and made him look at it. But then his face became more mask-like than ever, even his eyes wiped clean of expression.

'All right,' he said finally. 'You're a journalist.'

Sven gave a crow of laughter, but neither of them was looking at him.

Jordan said, 'Why me?'

'You're an interesting subject,' she said. 'A successful businessman who turned his back on the rat race.'

'There are others.'

'No . . . actually, most of the others are artists or entertainers, getting away from it all. And many of them only use their islands as holiday retreats. You've lived here for . . . six months, isn't it?'

'You've done some checking. Don't you know enough about me to write an article without . . . intruding on my privacy?'

She held her breath for an instant, then said steadily, 'No. I've very little information on the last two years. And I don't know why you're here or how long you intend to stay.'

'So you want to know about the last two years,' he said. His mouth twisted, and his eyes on her face were rapier keen.

'Yes.'

He held her eyes a moment longer, then got up and walked over to the shutters. He pushed one open, and the salt smell of the sea, mingled with the heavy perfumes of jasmine and frangipani, floated into the room. He turned, with the darkness behind him, and leaned on the sill, folding his arms. 'Tell me the real reason you're here,' he said.

His eyes were hard and cool, and she thought about passing Tila on the stairs, on her way to bed, and remembered how those hard eyes had softened for the island girl. 'I have told you,' she said. And then, very clearly and distinctly, she repeated, 'I'm doing a job.'

'Whose idea was this series?' he rapped out suddenly.

'My editor's.'

'And you jumped at the chance.'

'Of course. Anyone would; it's a very good chance.'

'How many islands have you visited so far?'

'Three,' she said, and rattled off their names and the names of the owners.

For a moment she thought she had surprised him. 'Prove it?' he suggested gently.

Sven made a brief sound of protest, but Keely said with great courtesy, born of triumph, 'Certainly.'

She turned to the table, flipped open the used notebook and handed it to him, then pressed down a switch on the tape recorder.

The fruity baritone of a very well-known actor came

clearly from the small speaker, then her own voice
asking a question and the actor answering her.

Jordan skimmed some of the notes she had made,
and then his head lifted and he listened, his mouth an
uncompromising line.

'Enough?' she asked, and he made an impatient
gesture with his hand.

She switched off the recorder, and a sudden silence
fell.

Sven said, 'There you are, Jordan. Give the girl a
break, why don't you?'

Jordan said nothing. He handed back the notebook
and turned to stare out into the night. Sven exchanged a
glance with Keely.

'Not tonight,' Jordan said, still with his back to them.

Keely took a quick, sharp breath. 'Tomorrow?' she
said.

'I'll be needed to finish the loading tomorrow.'
Jordan said. 'There won't be any time.'

'But we have to sail as soon as the loading is
completed,' Sven protested to the unmoving back. 'If
we wait about and bad weather comes up, we could be
stuck here for days.'

'Yes,' Jordan said. Then he turned around and said,
'So if Miss Alexander really wants this interview, she'll
just have to stay on, won't she?'

Sven looked astounded. 'Until our next run? But
that's a month away, Jordan!'

Jordan shrugged, and Sven looked suddenly angry.
This isn't like you, Jordan! You're being . . . deliberately difficult.'

'On the contrary, I'm being very accommodating.
The two of you won't take no for an answer. Well, Miss
Alexander can have her interview if she wants it badly
enough. When I have the time to give it to her. And I
don't have the time now. Take it or leave it.'

He was looking at her, and, without giving herself
time to think, she said, 'I'll take it.'

He gave no indication of pleasure or otherwise. She

didn't know if he had made the offer thinking she would turn it down or if he had some other motive. He simply said, 'Fine. Okay, Sven?'

His eyes challenged the other man. Sven looked doubtfully at Keely and shrugged in a discontented way.

'I usually take a stroll before I go to bed,' Jordan said. 'Will you two excuse me?'

When he had left, Keely began gathering up her things, and Sven said, 'Need any help?'

'No, thanks. I'll manage. You go ahead.'

She put her papers slowly back into the briefcase and ran the tape back to the beginning. She picked up the notebook that Jordan had looked at and put it in the briefcase with the other things. She stacked the coffee cups on the tray and was standing there, wondering if she should find the kitchen and wash them, when Jordan appeared in the doorway.

Her heart plunged as he closed the door behind him and stood against it, looking at her with his grey eyes dark and unfathomable.

'Want to change your mind?' he asked.

'No.'

'Tell me again why you decided to stay. Without a witness, this time.'

'You said,' she managed from a suddenly dry throat, 'it was the only way to get an interview.'

'That's the only reason?'

'Yes.'

He moved then, and she quivered as he came closer, his eyes holding hers. 'I think you're lying,' he said softly.

She couldn't answer. She knew what he was going to do before he put his hands on her shoulders, before his fingers bit into her flesh and dragged her towards him. She didn't even try to fight him when his mouth came down on hers and parted her lips in a hard, bruising kiss.

She didn't fight him, and she didn't respond, and

when he let her go, and said, '*Now* tell me!' she stepped
back from him with a pale, composed face and said,
'I'm not staying because of your overwhelming attraction for me, if that's what you think. I'm twenty-four
now, and a grown woman, not a teenager with a head
full of romantic dreams. And you don't turn me on in
the least. All I want from you is an interview and
permission to take a few photographs. Now, I'd like to
go to my room. Do you mind?'

For an instant he looked violent, his hands clenched
and dark colour running along his cheekbones. But he
controlled himself very quickly and said softly, 'I'll
come with you.'

'No!'

'Why not?' he demanded. 'I have the right—'

'As my host?' she challenged him.

'As your *husband*, damn you!' he said, furiously.
'Let's cut the pretence, shall we? There's nobody
around to know who you really are.'

'Who I really am,' she said deliberately, 'is Keely
Alexander, a journalist—on a job. Our marriage hasn't
existed, except on paper, for two years, Jordan. We've
both been getting along swimmingly without it, and I'm
not here as your wife, but, well, in a professional
capacity.'

It sounded vaguely pompous, and his lip curled in
sardonic amusement. 'Do you really expect me to
believe that?' he asked.

'I've furnished you with plenty of proof. Only a man
with an outsize ego would refuse to believe me.'

His eyes were narrow, his gaze on her face piercing,
but she met it without flinching. Behind the anger she
could see a hint of bafflement, and she felt a brief
spasm of satisfaction. Her coldness had shaken him,
and he hadn't liked the experience of being rejected,
for once. Had he thought she would fall into his arms?
Thank heaven she had remembered Tila, and her first
mad urge to respond to the touch of his hands and
mouth had died as quickly as it had flamed into life.

'Thanks,' Jordan said shortly. 'You'd better go upstairs before you get hurt—one way or another. I'm very tempted to strangle you, my lovely vixen.'

He flung open the door and watched with cold eyes as she passed him and went on up the stairs without looking back, glad that the long skirt of her dress hid her shaking legs.

Chapter Three

Sven tried to persuade Keely to change her mind, but the next day the *Alena* sailed without her.

She had watched the rest of the loading from the shore, taking pictures of the process after Jordan had given an uncaring shrug of permission. Careful not to get in the way, she photographed the bags stacked in the big storage sheds, and continued to take pictures as they were forklifted onto dusty trucks and transferred to the barges on pallets and taken through the reef to the ship. By late afternoon, the cargo was loaded and the ship weighed anchor and sailed away.

The islanders drifted off, and she carefully put her camera into its leather case and pushed the small notebook and pencil she had been using into the pocket of her cotton shirt.

Jordan and some of the other men had stripped off their shirts and dived into the lagoon to wash away their sweat and the yellow dust of the phosphate. He came over to her with his shirt slung over his shoulder, the brief shorts he wore plastered to his hips by the water, one hand pushing back seal-sleek hair. He reached into the Landrover and found a towel, rubbed his hair and face with it and then gave some cursory attention to the rest of his body. Then he tossed the towel in the back and said, 'Right. Let's go.'

She climbed into the passenger seat and he started the engine. As they moved along the road away from the quarry, she said, 'Do you mind if I ask questions while you drive?'

He cast her a quick glance and said, 'Depends what they are.'

'About the phosphate,' she said. 'Where does it come from—I mean, how is it formed?'

'Basically by bird droppings, over thousands of years. It lies in between pinnacles of coral and rock, covered by vegetation.'

'How much of it?'

'Plenty. It probably covers the entire island. It's good grade, too—finest quality stuff.'

'Then you've only just started?'

'The island has been mined since 1911. Some areas have been worked out.'

She took out her notebook, and he gave her a derisive glance and said, 'Are you still pretending to be a journalist?'

Quite evenly, she said, 'It's not pretence. What happens after an area is worked out?'

'You really want to know? I'll show you.'

He swung the wheel suddenly and they turned onto a side road that was so overgrown she hadn't noticed it. The Landrover bumped over a track on which tufts of grass grew, and Keely flinched as overhanging creepers slapped against the windscreen. They were climbing, and the trees to one side of them disappeared; she gasped as she realised the road was clinging to the slope of the mountain, with a sheer drop on the other side. Tangled dark growth seemed to fall away down the

mountainside and far below she could see the roofs of a
group of houses in a clearing.

They plunged into trees again, then came out on a
high plateau. Jordan braked and said, 'There you are.'

She felt cold shivers crawling up her spine. The sun
was setting, flaming in the sky near the horizon, and the
smoke from the *Alena's* stack hung lazily above the
black blur that was the ship. An eerie orange glow
added to the strangeness of the landscape spread before
them, a vista of oddly shaped white pinnacles and deep
hollows, a barren, stark, naked picture of desolation,
with no soil, no plants, no life.

It was such a contrast to the lushness of her first
view of the island that she glanced involuntarily down
to the green of the coastal flat below, and then back at
the bare plateau before her.

'How?' she asked finally.

'First the trees have to be bulldozed down,' Jordan
said. 'That's quite a job, because some of them are
hundreds of years old and up to a hundred and twenty
feet tall. It's rain forest, basically, and the trees have to
be stacked and dried out before they can be burnt.
After that, once the area is cleared, it's marked out in
grids and drilling starts. Then the excavators move in
and pull out the phosphate. It's trucked out to the
stockpiles you saw in the cove, the coral rock is
screened out and then it's dried and bagged, ready for
shipment.' He paused. 'Aren't you going to make
notes?' he asked, with a hint of sarcasm.

'I'll remember. Is the phosphate worth—' she gestured to the desolation in front of them— 'all this?'

'Phosphate is a very valuable fertiliser.'

'I suppose you've made a lot of money out of this
island.'

After a short silence, he said, 'My company has.'

'But you *are* the company! Or you were, before
you decided to throw it all in and become a beachcomber.'

She saw his hand tighten on the steering wheel, and a tiny muscle flickered into life along his jaw. He wasn't looking at her but gazing out over the plateau. Rashly, she said, 'Or are you overseeing your investment? Is that why you came here?'

He looked at her then, his eyes holding a glint that she couldn't read. 'You said you wanted to ask questions about the phosphate,' he said. 'We'll leave my motives out of it for now.'

They drove back to the main track in silence, and as he pulled up outside the house the brief twilight ended and the tropical night enveloped them.

'We've been invited to a party tonight,' Jordan said as she moved to get out. 'A Fijian *magiti*.'

"We . . . ?'

'It's in your honour,' he said. 'And also to celebrate the successful loading.'

'What time?' she asked.

'I'll give you an hour to get ready. It's informal, but wear a dress or skirt.'

She showered and changed into a white silk blouse with tiny pearl buttons down the front and a flared skirt with white daisies printed on a navy background. Her hair had been pinned up all day, and she brushed it out and left it loose, then slipped her feet into a pair of wedge-heeled raffia sandals. Her face looked a little pinched, and she used rather more makeup than usual, taking care with the eye shadow to accentuate the green of her eyes and applying a coral pink lipstick to her mouth.

When she went down the stairs Jordan came out of the lounge, dressed in a white open-necked shirt and dark trousers. He held a large electric torch in his hand. He said, 'Do you mind walking? It isn't far, and we conserve petrol as much as we can here.'

'I don't mind,' she said, and they went out together into the scented night, under a sky laden with brilliant stars.

Jordan switched on the torch and led her down to the beach where she had landed only yesterday, and they walked along the crisp sand for a while with the moonlit water whispering softly to shore a few yards away. Then he touched her arm and said, 'Over here,' and she saw a narrow pathway leading into the trees and heard voices not far away, along with the hollow note of a bamboo drum.

They suddenly came out of the darkness into a vast circle of light, and a peculiarly harmonious cry of welcome went up as Keely blinked at the rough semicircle of thatched, traditional *bures* and the two or three square, European-style buildings roofed with corrugated iron. People in brightly coloured shirts, blouses and wraparound *sulus* seemed to be milling about, but a small group broke away and led them into the firelit circle. There were flares, too, burning dangerously close, Keely thought, to some of the thatched roofs. Kerosine lamps added to the brightness.

Woven mats and cushions were spread in front of one of the larger houses, and Jordan and Keely were seated side by side and surrounded by smiling men and women, while dark-eyed children peeped curiously over their elders' shoulders and giggled and ran away.

'Who is the chief?' Keely asked Jordan in a whisper, not wanting to slight that important personage by not according him the proper greetings and courtesies.

'There is no hereditary chieftainship on Salutu,' he said quietly. 'Give this to the elderly gentleman in the red sulu. He's one of the leading lights of the island council."

He pushed a small packet into her palm as the dignified islander approached to shake them by the hand, and she obeyed. She knew by the way it felt that it was *yaqona* root, to be made into the ceremonial drink for the formal welcome ceremony.

Everyone sat quietly while this solemn part of the proceedings was carried out, and Jordan murmured in

Keely's ear, as the old man carefully squeezed juice from a handful of roots, 'Once it was made by young girls chewing the root and spitting the juice into a bowl. The health inspectors put a stop to that.'

Eventually they were handed coconut shells full of the cloudy liquid, and Keely fancied she caught a gleam of approval in Jordan's eyes as she bravely drained hers in the proper fashion.

She was a little alarmed when she was offered a second cup of the potent stuff, and she took care to drink it more slowly. Jordan had three cups and seemed to enjoy them, and other members of the 'official party' were dipping into the big wooden bowl, the *tanoa,* so that the level went down quite quickly. When the *tanoa* was at last empty, the solemnity of the ritual dropped away, and laughter and chatter accompanied the serving of what seemed like mountains of food—a whole roast pig, fish cooked in coconut sauce, *kasava,* Indian *roti,* like spicy pancakes wrapped around curried meat and vegetables, starchy *daro* root, yams and bananas in a variety of dishes and a sweet pudding called *vakalolo,* the ingredients of which she could not even guess at.

Keely had shaken hands with so many people that her fingers ached and her head reeled with the musical strangeness of their names. She had recognised a few of the women from the beach yesterday, and Tila was present, helping to distribute the food. She looked particularly lovely in a yellow sulu printed with red flowers and a brief matching top, her dark hair a perfect background for the scarlet hibiscus blossom above one ear.

Keely was very conscious of Jordan sitting at her side, and when his arm brushed hers as he moved to help himself to a bowl of marinated raw fish, she moved sharply, causing him to cast her a curious, faintly amused glance.

She said hastily, to cover the moment, 'Is this the island's entire population?'

'Virtually,' he answered. 'This is the only settlement of any size. The island is less than twenty square miles in area. The population amounts to about a thousand people altogether.

One of the elders clapped his hands and called out, and a group of young girls dressed in stiff gathered skirts of cream and brown patterned tapa cloth, with wide white sashes tied in enormous bows at the back, moved into the central area in front of them. Garlands of leaves and wild flowers adorned the girls' black hair and colourful bracelets of dyed feathers encircled their wrists. They swung immediately into a synchronised dance accompanied by their own beautifully harmonised singing, the first song followed by two more numbers in varying tempos.

A group of men then got to their feet and performed a breathtaking, literally earthshaking dance using lighted brands, which they whirled until sparks flew wildly and passed with apparently effortless skill from hand to hand as they stamped and pranced in the complicated figures of the dance.

More singing followed, accompanied by drums and guitars, ukuleles and sometimes simple handclapping, and then the clacking of the bamboo drums quickened and Tila moved into the circle of people with her hips swaying and her hands moving gracefully. She was followed by a handsome young man dressed in a blue and white flowered sulu and a lei of tropical flowers. Encouraged by applause and appreciative comments from the audience, the couple danced a supple, sensuous Tahitian *tamuré*. Watching the flirtatious gestures of their hands and the explicit movements of their bodies as they flashed gleaming smiles at each other, Keely didn't wonder that the early missionaries had found the *tamuré* shocking and tried to suppress it.

'I don't think you need a translation of this,' Jordan said dryly in her ear as the dance came to an exciting climax and the panting performers, hand in hand, laughed triumphantly at their ecstatic audience. Tila's flower had fallen from her hair, and her partner picked up the scarlet blossom from the hard, dusty ground and tucked it into his own tight curls, causing laughter and more applause.

The formal part of the entertainment seemed to have come to an end, and now a dozen couples were dancing to a melody Keely recognised as a pop tune of several years ago.

Tila and her dancing partner appeared in front of Jordan and Keely, and the young man gave her a meaningful look, his dark eyebrows raised.

Jordan said, 'Kanimea is asking you to dance.'

Taken aback, Keely hesitated. She wasn't sure what kind of dancing the islander had in mind. Then she saw that Tila was smiling at Jordan, directing at him the same silent invitation, and she was suddenly sure that she didn't want to be sitting here like a wallflower while Jordan danced with the pretty Salutuan girl.

She smiled and got to her feet, and her partner led her in among the dancers and began teaching her, with a wide grin, something that seemed very like disco dancing. She soon picked up the simple steps and began to enjoy herself. She didn't look round to see Jordan dancing with Tila—she didn't want to.

The music changed and another young man swept her into a very correct ballroom hold and they waltzed sedately for several minutes. Keely didn't see Jordan, and she wondered, with a sudden suffocating pang, if he had slipped off into the trees with Tila.

But moments later he was by her side, his hand on her waist as the dancers formed a ring with their arms about each other and began a new series of steps on which she had to concentrate to follow. It was simple enough and she soon picked up the rhythm, but she was terribly conscious of the hard warmth of Jordan's arm and conscious, also, that his other arm encircled Tila's slim waist.

But when the circle broke, Tila was swept away by Kanimea, her partner from the *tamuré*, and Keely found herself dancing as if in a nightclub back home, with both of Jordan's hands at her waist and hers imprisoned against his chest.

She felt the hardness of his chest under her palms, his breath stirring her hair against her temple, his thighs moving against hers in time to the music. A feverish excitement stirred her blood, and she closed her eyes and slid her hands up around his neck until his hair brushed the tips of her fingers. His hands tightened on her and began moving, stroking her back, and the flickering firelight that had danced against her closed lids suddenly turned to blackness as he stopped moving. She opened her eyes to find that he had danced her into the deep black shadows of the palms.

His hands on her back burned through the silk blouse, and, as she tipped back her head, trying to find his eyes in the darkness, she heard him draw a harsh breath. Then her eyes closed as he found her parted lips with his in a kiss of blinding passion, curving her body ruthlessly over his arm as he pulled her closer to his own, while the other hand found her breast and rested there possessively.

When he released her mouth she gasped in a shuddering breath, and gasped again as his lips touched burningly on her throat and moved down to the open neck of her blouse, his fingers impatiently pulling at the tiny buttons to give his mouth access to the gentle curve of her breast.

The throbbing beat of the drums and the thud of the dancers' footsteps were at one with the beating of her heart as his hand pressed over it, but the music suddenly stopped. In the lull she heard a clear feminine laugh that she was certain belonged to Tila.

Sanity returned abruptly, and she began to struggle against the hands that held her. 'Jordan—*no!*' she said in a choking whisper. 'Don't!'

He raised his head slowly, and said, 'All right. Not here—not now.'

Someone called his name, and his hands relaxed so that she could pull away. She turned and stumbled in the direction of the firelight, and as he came after her she thought he said, 'Later, Keely.'

She fumbled with her buttons, doing them up before she moved into the light. She hovered at the edge of the trees, in the shadow, as Jordan sauntered forward and walked away from her with a group of islanders.

She returned slowly to the pile of mats and cushions where the elders still sat and managed to convey her thanks for the *magiti* and her appreciation of the effort they had put into entertaining her. She wondered how soon she could ask Jordan to take her back to the house without seeming impolite. Then she realised that the request might make it seem as though she was anxious to take up where they had left off, just now. Her cheeks burned with the memory, and she shivered. Did he really think she would fall into his arms so readily? She must have been mad, letting him kiss her like that, touch her as he had.

Her eyes found him talking to Tila and the young man Kanimea. She saw him smile, as though amused at something Tila said, and then turn away, coming towards Keely and the elders. Tila put her hand on Kanimea's arm briefly, and he shrugged and walked off in the other direction, looking rather disgruntled. And then Tila came after Jordan, catching up with him as he reached Keely.

He turned to smile at her before he spoke to Keely. 'We're ready to go, if you are.'

Her stomach churning with emotion, Keely kept her voice cool and steady.

'Of course,' she said, and stood up gracefully, ignoring the hand he held out to her. She thanked the elders again and the three of them left together, Jordan walking between the girls at first, then going ahead of them with the torch and shining it on the rough path for them.

'I hope you enjoyed yourself, *marama,*' Tila said as they neared the white sand of the beach, glimmering softly in the moonlight.

Keely unclenched her teeth and said, 'Very much, thank you.'

'Kanimea said you are a good dancer.'

'Not as good as you,' Keely said politely.

Tila laughed. 'Thank you. I will teach you the *tamuré* if you like. It isn't difficult.'

'Thank you, but I don't think I'd be very good at it.'

'Why not? You have a sense of rhythm, and the figure—*nice bola!*'

'What?'

'Beautiful, Keely,' Jordan translated. 'Why don't you think you'd be good at it? Are you afraid you're too inhibited for it?'

'Maybe I am,' she said.

He suddenly flashed the torch up to her face, so that she blinked and turned away in protest, nearly colliding with him because he had suddenly stopped walking.

'I doubt it,' he said softly, and then, 'Here's the path to the house. Watch your step.'

I will, she thought grimly. *I certainly will.* But she wasn't thinking about the dark path through the trees at all.

She went straight up to her room, saying goodnight to them both very clearly. She visited the bathroom briefly, then undressed and quickly pulled her cotton nightdress on and brushed her hair, determined that she was not going to listen for the sounds of Jordan and Tila coming up and going to their rooms—or room.

Fiercely, she pulled the brush over her scalp, trying to block out thought. Someone came up the stairs and she heard a door snap open and shut. She put the brush down with a clatter on the dressing table, seeing her face in the mirror above, pale and shadowed about the

eyes. There was a pink mark on her throat, and she
touched it with her fingers, then almost unwillingly slid
aside the strap of her nightdress, exposing, on the white
curve of her breast, another small reddened blotch.
Sudden heat ran through her body as she recalled the
rough passion of Jordan's mouth on her skin.

Later, he had said. But surely Tila was with him
now—he wouldn't . . . ?

Her knees trembled as she went to switch off the
light. The door had a brightly polished brass handle and
beneath it was an old fashioned lock with a long key in
it. She turned it, and it made a loud click as it went
home. For a few moments she stood with her hand still
on it, then switched off the light and crossed the
moonlit room to the high brass bed.

Someone walked past her door, and she heard a door
further down the passageway open and close. The
same—or a different one? She didn't know. But a long
time later she heard soft footfalls again and sat up, her
heart pounding. She could see the gleam of the brass
doorknob as the moonlight caught it. The gleam shifted
as the handle turned, just once, and she heard the faint
sound of the latch.

Her hand was clutching the sheet tightly and she held
her breath. There was a muffled thump as someone
pushed strongly at the door, then a long silence before
the footsteps went softly away.

In the morning she woke heavy-eyed, with an acute
sense of depression. She splashed her face repeatedly
with cold water in the bathroom and spent some time
covering the evidence of a restless night with makeup.

She donned a denim skirt and blouse that looked
crisp and workmanlike and made her way downstairs.
No one seemed to be about, and she hesitated as she
reached the hall. The wide front door was open and the
sun gleamed on the sea that she glimpsed through the
dark palms and breadfruit trees.

Drawn by the dreaming beauty of the view, she

moved to the doorway and saw Jordan emerging from
the path to the beach, dressed in dark swim shorts with
a towel slung about his neck.

Quelling the urge to retreat into the house, she
waited for him. His eyes caught hers before he reached
the steps and held them silently until he was almost at
the door. His hair was damp from his swim and small
droplets of water gleamed in the dark curls of hair on
his chest.

She said, 'Good morning. Did you enjoy your swim?'

He stopped in front of her, his eyes sombre and a
little impatient. 'Yes!' he said, and seemed to hesitate
before he added, rather abruptly, 'Have you had
breakfast?'

'I've only just come down.'

'I usually have mine on the terrace out back. Will you
wait for me?'

'Of course. You're my host.'

Anger tightened his lips, but he said only, 'I won't
keep you waiting long. There's a side door just beyond
the stairs. Can you find your way?'

She did, walking through the glass door onto a tiled
area with fragrant creepers creating a sort of openwork
roof supported by white-painted columns and beams,
dappling the morning sun. A round table was set where
the sun slanted in from the east, and Tila was standing
by it, arranging spoons and glasses.

She turned and smiled at Keely, and Keely forced
her stiff mouth to respond.

Tila said, 'Good morning. Jordan won't be long.'

'I know. I met him as I came down.'

'Did you sleep well?'

Keely clenched her teeth, momentarily tempted to
ask, *Did you?* Then she said woodenly, 'I was very
comfortable, thank you.'

'Good.'

There was a silence, and Keely walked to the edge of
the terrace. From there, a glimpse of the blue sea was
visible beyond the corner of the house, and behind the

terrace a grassed slope ran under thick trees. The constant gentle shushing of the waves made a background to the birdcalls coming from the trees, but there seemed to be another sound closer at hand. Keely said, 'Can I hear a waterfall?'

'There is a waterfall not far through the trees.' Tila moved over to her and pointed. 'You can just see a glimpse of it, there—see?'

A moving silvery gleam showed through the thick foliage of the trees, and Keely said, 'Yes. I can see it now.'

'I think the island was named for that waterfall,' Tila said. 'You must get Jordan to show it to you. It's very pretty.'

'What does Salutu mean?' Keely asked.

'It is thought to be a shortening of *Sa-lutu-tengu-ni-mataka,* meaning "Falling tears of the morning."'

'That's lovely!' Keely exclaimed.

'And sad, too, I think,' Tila said.

Lovely and sad, Keely thought. Did that describe the island?

Jordan came out onto the terrace and they turned simultaneously to face him. He was wearing sand-coloured lightweight trousers that hugged his hips and powerful thighs and a cream shirt left open at his brown throat. He looked very masculine and vital, and he smiled at them easily and said unexpectedly, 'Midnight and morning!'

Keely hardly heard him; she was expending a lot of energy on looking cool and self-possessed. But Tila moved towards him and said with a lilt of laughter in her voice, 'What are you talking about, Jordan?'

'You and Keely,' he said, smiling down at her. 'You're both beautiful women, in striking contrast, especially the colour of your hair when you stand in the morning sun together.' He glanced down and a flicker of something crossed his face before he looked up again and said lightly, 'I'm a fortunate man, having such lovely company for breakfast.'

Keely turned away to hide a sudden rush of fury.
Jordan said, 'Won't you sit down, Keely?' and she had
to pause a moment before turning to take the chair he
was holding out for her. Tila was already seated, taking
the shell-weighted circle of net from a glass jug, and
pouring pure orange juice into their glasses.

There was a bowl of bananas and mangoes and huge
papayas, their almost cloying sweetness relieved by a
sprinling of lemon juice. Keely found herself surprisingly hungry.

Jordan and Tila exchanged a few remarks about the
previous evening's entertainment. Tila seeming very
amused about someone called Ilai who had, she said
with a soft giggle, been 'kasou.'

Jordan looked at her dancing eyes with a crinkling at
the corners of his own, although his mouth remained
grave. 'Ilai?' he said. 'Don't be so disrespectful, Tila.
I'm sure he's never been drunk in his life!'

'I don't think he has ever danced the vude before,
either,' Tila said. 'Usually he sits and looks disapprov-
ing, like this!' She turned her pretty mouth down at the
corners and scowled, and Jordan broke into a shout of
laughter.

Keely's hand tightened on the spoon she had been
using to scoop out the firm sweet flesh of her papaya,
and then she suddenly put it down and pushed back her
chair. She couldn't bear to watch the two of them any
longer.

Tila turned smiling dark eyes to her. 'Have you had
sufficient, marama?' she asked.

'Thank you, yes,' Keely answered with difficulty. 'It
was quite delicious.'

Jordan looked at her sharply and said to Tila, 'Her
name is Keely. She won't mind if you call her by it.'

Keely turned on him a look of pure hatred that
brought a quick frown to his eyes, and with an effort
she stopped herself from snapping I would mind very
much! How dared he make assumptions like that on her
behalf? But she stopped the words in time. After all,

she had no desire to hurt Tila; Jordan was the one at fault.

There was a short, strained silence, and Tila said, 'Would you like coffee?'

'No, thank you.'

Tila got up and, without looking at Keely, began to clear away the used dishes.

Heavens! Keely thought. *What a cat she must think I am!* She got up quickly and said, 'Let me help you.'

Tila shot her a surprised, wary look, and Keely said, 'Please!'

'I told you,' Jordan said abruptly, 'Tila doesn't like visitors in the kitchen. Or men—' he added, shooting a meaningful smile at the island girl. She responded with a soft laugh, and a shaft of pain shot through Keely as she realised that they were sharing an old joke, and a private one.

'Jordan is right,' Tila said, smiling apologetically but with a hint of reserve at Keely. 'I can manage better on my own. But thank you for offering to help.'

Jordan went to open the door for Tila as she passed through with her hands full. Keely would have followed her, but Jordan had closed the door and taken a couple of paces back onto the terrace, effectively blocking her exit.

His eyes looked hard and watchful, and as he thrust his hands into his pockets, rocking a little on his heels, she said quickly, 'Do you think we could get on with that interview today? If you're not too busy.'

As always, the mention of her reason for coming to Salutu brought an angry light to the grey eyes. But he said evenly, 'As it's Sunday, and the islanders keep a very quiet Sabbath, I expect we might, if you're still insisting on it.'

'If I'm going to be stuck here for a month,' she said rather waspishly, 'I certainly do insist on having something to show for it.'

His mouth went grim and the hands in his pockets balled into fists. 'Then we might as well get it out of the

way,' he said. 'I don't imagine your readers want a
great deal of detail.'

'Why should you think that?' she asked, trying not to
show annoyance.

'What you're doing is basically a travelogue with a bit
of human interest thrown in, isn't it? You're not exactly
in the investigative reporting business.'

He *meant* to be insulting—she knew it. But losing her
temper with him would only play into his hands. She
looked into his eyes with cool dislike and said, 'Not
exactly. But you'll find out, won't you?'

'Supposing I've changed my mind?'

'Why should you? Are you afraid of what I might
uncover?' she taunted.

She had known that would sting, but the only sign of
it was a slight narrowing of his eyes.

'I have nothing to be afraid of,' he said, with slight
scorn.

'Then you won't mind answering questions, will
you?'

'What are you trying to do?' he said scoffingly. 'Scare
me?'

'You just said you've nothing to be scared of.'

'That's right. And what about you? Why did you lock
your door last night?'

He caught her unaware with the unexpected question, but she recovered her composure very quickly and
said, 'If you know that it was locked, then you must
know why I locked it.'

He took a step towards her, and as she made to move
back he put out his hand and caught her arm, his fingers
steely strong on her skin. 'Keely—' he said. And then
the door behind him opened and Tila stood in the
doorway, surprise and uncertainty in her face as he
turned a blackly frowning look on her.

She was dressed in a short pink cotton frock that
formed a tunic over a pink and white floral long skirt
with a deep slit in the front, and wore a white *broderie*

anglaise jacket and a little straw boater style hat garlanded with fresh flowers. 'I came to tell you I'm going to church now, Jordan,' she said, her face faintly troubled.

Jordan released Keely and turned an expressionless face to the other girl. 'Okay, Tila,' he said. 'Thank you.'

Keely, suddenly panicked at the realisation that she and Jordan would be alone in the big house, walked quickly past him and said, 'May I come with you, Tila?'

Surprised, Tila said, 'Yes, of course. Why don't you come, too, Jordan?'

He gave her a tight smile and said, 'Some other time.'

Tila shook her head and told Keely, 'He always says that. Only twice have I known him to come.'

Keely's answering smile was strained. She was bitterly noting this further evidence of their intimacy. 'Should I change?' she asked, her eyes on the other girl's formal attire that was vaguely reminiscent of a Victorian print.

'Oh, no!' Tila smiled. 'Just . . . something for your head, perhaps?'

'Will a scarf do?'

'Yes, certainly.'

Keely ran up the stairs and came down again with a bright red and black printed triangle tied gypsy-fashion over her hair. Tila and Jordan were standing in the hall in front of the door, and Tila looked less serene than usual, her white teeth biting into her full lower lip and her eyes puzzled. Jordan put his hand on her shoulder with a gentle touch and smiled, but there was more than a trace of arrogance in the tilt of his head. Although he spoke too quietly for Keely to hear what he was saying, she recognised a note of suppressed impatience in his voice.

Anger shot through Keely again. She ran down the last three stairs and showed Tila the camera in her hand. 'I don't suppose I should take pictures in church,' she said, 'but will anyone mind if I photograph them going in and coming out?'

'I'm sure they won't.'

Tila cast a look of appeal at Jordan, but he ignored it and turned abruptly back into the house as the two girls went down the steps and made for the path. As they entered the cool, rustling grove of trees, Tila said, 'Jordan is not himself this morning, I think. Maybe he had a little too much to drink last night, like Ilai.' Her eyes went to Keely's bare arm where faint pink marks showed from Jordan's ungentle grip, and she said, 'He would never deliberately hurt anyone.'

Wouldn't he? Keely thought cynically. The girl must be blindly in love. She was probably so sweet and biddable that he had never hurt her in any way—yet. But he wouldn't think twice about it if she ever crossed his will—or showed she had a mind of her own.

'You really don't have to make excuses for him to me, Tila,' she said, a little sharply. 'And don't worry about me, either, please. I'm quite capable of sticking up for myself.'

Tila looked away and said hurriedly, 'Yes, *marama.* I'm sorry.'

Oh, no! Keely thought, dismayed. *Did I really sound like the memsahib reprimanding the maidservant?*

'I didn't mean it like that,' she said. 'And please call me Keely. I'd like you to.'

Tila looked at her doubtfully, as though testing her sincerity, and then smiled widely, with a hint of mischief. 'I think I was silly this morning,' she said. 'Last night you were so friendly with everyone, but at breakfast, I thought you didn't like me because I'm an islander.'

Keely flushed with distress and said, 'It wasn't *that!* I mean—you were mistaken, Tila, honestly!'

'I think you wanted to have breakfast alone with Jordan, eh?' Tila slanted her a sly smile.

'*No!*'

Tila smiled as though she didn't believe it, and said, 'You like Jordan, though?'

'Not especially,' Keely said. 'No.'

Tila shot her a strange, laughing look. 'No? Oh, well . . .' She shrugged rather elaborately. 'That's okay.'

Nonplussed, Keely couldn't imagine what to say. Then they arrived at the settlement, which in daylight was much bigger than she had imagined. The church was a wooden building with a corrugated iron roof and plain glass windows but decorated inside with painted tapa cloth and beautifully woven palm-leaf mats patterned with bright wool.

The service was conducted in Fijian by a solemn-faced, middle-aged islander with great dignity and decorum, and when Tila whispered to her, 'Did you meet Ilai last night?' and nodded towards him with mischief in her smile, Keely realised why Ilai's immoderate consumption at the *magiti* had so appealed to the Salutuan girl's sense of humour.

Keely photographed Ilai in front of the church after the service and snapped some of the children dressed in their Sunday clothes, snowy shirts and coloured shorts on the boys and starched cotton dresses on the girls. The adults posed graciously when she asked them, dignified and, she thought, surely rather hot in their suits and flowing dresses, and she got some shots of colourful groups gossiping as they made their leisurely way to their homes.

Tila said, 'I will not return to the big house with you, Keely. I shall spend the day with my family. You are welcome to visit us if you would like to.'

'Jordan promised he would give me the interview I came for today. May I take you up on your invitation another time?'

'Of course. Can you find your way back? I can send someone with you, if you like.'

'No, I'll be fine. I want to take some photographs on the way, in any case.'

She took a couple of close-ups of tiny, fragile red flowers on the way back, and a shot of the beach framed by coconut palms—a cliché shot, she admitted wryly, but one hard to resist.

She half expected to find Jordan waiting for her at the door; he must have a fairly good idea what time the service finished. But the house was silent and seemed empty. There was nobody in the lounge or on the terrace where they had breakfasted. She hadn't been particularly quiet, and if he was lurking in one of the rooms she had not yet seen, he must have heard her.

Perhaps he had gone out, she thought, making for the stairs. She would put her scarf and camera in her room and go downstairs again and wait. He would have to come back sometime.

She pulled off the scarf as she opened the door of her room, closing it behind her, and, as she shook out her hair, turned to put the camera down on the dressing table. She glanced in the mirror and gasped, her whole body quivering with shock. The bed was reflected in the mirror, and she could see that the mosquito net had been pulled back and the cover folded down. And she also saw the shirt carelessly thrown over the brass bed end, the sandals lying on the dark polished wood of the floor and the man lying on the bed with his long legs, clad in sand-coloured trousers, almost touching the foot of it, his dark head cradled comfortably in his hands on the pillow and his cynical grey eyes meeting her startled stare in the mirror.

Chapter Four

Keely whipped round so fast that she had to steady herself with a hand on the edge of the dressing table behind her. *'What are you doing here?'* she demanded.

Jordan turned his head a little further and raised an eyebrow at her. 'Waiting for you, of course, darling.'

'Don't call me that!' she said furiously.

'Why not?'

'You know why not! And will you please get out of my room—and take your clothes with you!'

He didn't answer or move, except for his eyes, which were slowly inspecting her, mentally stripping her, and he obviously didn't care if she knew it.

A hot flare of anger rose in her, and her fingers curled around the handle of the hairbrush lying on the dressing table as he suddenly swung off the bed and came towards her. He was smiling, but his movements had the silent grace of a predator.

'Don't you dare touch me!' she said breathlessly.

His smile became a grin as he drew closer. She saw

his arm tense, and she immediately lifted the brush in her clenched hand.

He moved so fast she didn't know how it happened. His hand clamped onto her wrist and twisted, and she gave a cry of pain as the hairbrush clattered to the floor. Before she had time to recover from that, he had picked her up in his arms and was striding towards the bed. She kicked out wildly, but he tossed her onto the mattress and held her down, his hands on her wrists, one knee on the bed beside her as he bent over her. 'I'll touch you if and when I want to, Keely,' he said. 'You didn't mind so much last night.'

She stopped struggling—it was useless, anyway—and looked up with blazing eyes into his dark face. 'Last night,' she said, 'I had a lot more *yaqona* than I'm used to, and I was—affected by the dancing. This morning I'm of sound mind, and I *loathe* you, Jordan Lang! I haven't wanted you for years!'

'You kissed me back—'

'In that mood, I'd have kissed any man back!' she said. 'I'm not yet accustomed to tropical moonlight and the *tamuré*.'

'You wanted *me*. You couldn't hide it.'

'It wore off,' Keely said, 'with the *yaqona*.' She forced herself to look at him calmly, her eyes flickering over the taut jaw, the bare, suntanned chest, the muscular arms that still held her. 'In daylight,' she said deliberately, 'I don't find you nearly so . . . interesting.'

Dark anger smouldered in his eyes and he said gratingly, 'We'll see—'

She made one instinctive, futile attempt to escape as he moved and pulled her roughly to him, but he dealt with it without compunction, one arm about her with his fingers biting into her shoulder and the other hand holding her nape as his merciless kiss bent her head back until her neck hurt.

The pain helped her to withold the response he wanted. She knew that struggling would make him even more ruthless, and she willed herself to lie still and not feel a thing.

For long moments his mouth possessed hers with a cruel hunger, bruising her lips. Then he seemed to go still, and she thought with relief that he would let her go. Instead, the kiss changed, as though he had checked his anger and decided on a different tactic. His lips became soft and coaxing, and, although his hands still held her firmly, his thumb began caressing her throat and teasing gently at her earlobe.

Keely stiffened, and when his hand moved from her neck to follow the curve of her back to the roundness of her hips, she jerked her head aside, wordlessly rejecting him.

His fingers raked into her loosened hair and forced her round again to face him, her eyes alight with anger. His mouth came down again with punishing force, draining her strength. She closed her eyes tightly and a kaleidoscope of light danced behind her lids.

Then suddenly she was free, slumping back dizzily against the pillow, gasping for breath, and Jordan, his breathing hard and uneven, was standing by the bed with violence in his eyes. 'You're quite a girl, aren't you?' he said harshly. 'Instant frigidity at will. It's a clever trick.'

'It isn't a trick,' she said, turning away from him. 'I don't want you anymore, Jordan. Is it too hard on your masculine ego to accept that?'

'I don't accept things I don't like,' he said. 'I change them.'

How typical of him that was, she thought. She sat up and slid off the bed to face him, her eyes flashing defiance. 'You can't change people to suit yourself,' she said. 'I would have thought you'd have learned that by now!'

His eyes glinted, but instead of speaking he turned his head suddenly, his attitude alert and listening.

Keely was at a loss until she heard the sounds that he had evidently noticed before she did—a child's high, terrified screaming, and another voice, also childish, calling out something she couldn't quite catch.

Jordan went to the window and thrust the shutter wide, looking down. Then he gave a sudden low exclamation and without another word strode over to the door and, leaving it open, ran down the stairs.

After a moment of bewilderment, Keely followed. Jordan was halfway across the front hall as she got to the top of the stairs, and when she reached the bottom he was already coming into the house again, with a small, dark, crying child in his arms and another following at his heels.

'Get the first-aid kit from the bathroom cupboard, Keely,' he said, and she flew to obey, snatching the box and a couple of towels and returning to find he had set the little boy down on one of the loungers in the front room.

There seemed to be a lot of blood, but as he gently bathed the wound, speaking soothingly all the while to the boy, she was relieved to see that there was only a small cut causing it, just under the hairline on the child's forehead.

It was soon cleaned, disinfected and dressed, and Jordan sent the two children on their way with some remark in Fijian that made them grin happily.

'It seems he fell from a tree and sensibly came here for help as it's closer than the village,' he said. 'Well—crisis over.'

The glint in his eye might have been slightly derisive, and she wasn't certain which crisis he meant. Then he grimaced at the bloodstains on his trousers and hands and said, 'I'd better get cleaned up. Better still, I'll get these clothes off and have a swim. Care to join me?'

Keely scarcely hesitated. She felt hot and wrought up after the drama of the last half hour. 'Yes, please,' she said.

The water received them warmly, seeming to embrace their almost naked bodies with a loving, caressing touch as they went into it. Keely swam lazily, and Jordan for a time literally made rings around her, his powerful arms stroking with econonomy and speed.

Keely turned on her back and floated, watching insubstantial streaks of white cloud hovering against the azure sky and the tops of the coconut palms on the shore moving in the slight warm breeze.

Jordan's sleek black head broke the water nearby and he grinned at her, his eyes wicked and teasing. 'You look very tempting from below,' he said. 'Just as well there are no sharks in the lagoon.'

'Aren't there?' she asked, deliberately dry.

He laughed and said, 'Don't tempt fate.' Then he turned on his back to float beside her. Softly, he said, 'How do you like my island, Keely?'

'Why do you want to know?' she asked.

'Why shouldn't I?' he countered. 'How would you like to stay here and live with me?'

Keely suddenly turned, treading water so that she could stare into his face. He was smiling, his teeth white against his tan, his eyes crinkled against the glare from the sky, a teasing light in them.

With a sudden, consuming desire to wipe the smile off his face, she reached out and put a hand on his chest, pushing him under.

His hand grabbed her wrist even before he twisted himself round and came up for air, and she automatically took a breath as he reached for her with the other hand, his eyes sparkling a warning.

But instead of retaliating in kind, he pulled her close and kissed her, a salty, hard kiss on her unwilling mouth. She kicked against him and then they both sank under the water. She felt her legs slipping against the muscular warmth of his and was suddenly hotly aware of the brevity of her black, satiny bikini as his hands hauled her closer.

For a moment longer he held her lips with his, then let her go. She broke the surface and turned to swim swiftly to the beach.

Two towels and the black and white sulu she had worn, sarong-fashion, before going in the water lay on the white sand. She sank down on one of the towels, lying prone with her eyes closed against her folded arms.

Her skin prickled with awareness when Jordan came to sit beside her, but she lay perfectly still.

A hand touched her dripping ponytail, then tugged at the elastic band which held it, and spread the wet strands over her back. She felt the softness of a towel against her shoulders and realised that Jordan was carefully drying her hair.

When he stopped, she held her breath expectantly, but nothing happened, and she gradually relaxed and let the sun soothe her into drowsiness.

She was half asleep when Jordan gently shook her. 'Come on,' he said. 'You can't lie about in this sun too long.' And even though she was barely awake, she knew that the brief warmth at the curve of her neck was the fleeting caress of his lips. But when she rolled over he was sitting two feet from her on the sand, tossing a small spiral shell in his hand.

Keely sat up, shook back her hair and said, 'Where's my hair tie?'

'I like it better loose.'

He wasn't going to give it to her, had probably thrown it away. What was the use of starting another argument? Resignedly, she got up, donned her sulu, shook out her towel and started for the path to the house.

Jordan was right behind her. As they reached the house, he said, 'Lunch in twenty minutes, okay?'

The meal was cold and delicious, and although Jordan vetoed her offer to wash up, she followed him into the gleaming, up-to-date kitchen. 'Did you have it modernised?' she asked.

'If you mean since I came here, no. The company did, some years back.'

'Who was living here then?'

'An agent of the company. Are these questions in your professional capacity or your personal one?'

'I was just curious. But you did promise me an interview. Could we do it now?'

His mouth compressed for a moment, but his voice was emotionless as he said, 'If you must play out this farce, now is as good a time as any.'

'It's no farce,' she said, keeping her voice quiet. 'I really want that interview. I really am writing that book. I thought I'd proved that.'

'All right,' he said, with a flicker of irritation. 'Go and get your notebook, or whatever you need. I'll be in the lounge.'

When she came down, holding her tape recorder, notebook and pencil, he was standing before the open shutters, staring out at the sea. 'Where would you like to sit?' she asked him, adopting a briskly professional manner that made his eyes narrow unpleasantly. 'I like the subject to be comfortable,' she explained kindly.

'I don't care,' he said. 'Would you like a drink?'

'No, thank you. But if you need one, go ahead, by all means.'

She put her things down on one of the low tables and sat on a cushioned chair. Jordan cast her a glance of dislike and seated himself opposite her.

'Will it bother you if I record the conversation?' she asked him politely.

'No,' he said shortly.

'Good. Being recorded makes some people nervous,' she explained.

Jordan didn't bother to comment on that. *She* was suddenly horribly nervous herself, her fingers shaking a little as she pressed the record button and picked up her notebook and pencil. She resisted the urge to wipe her damp palm against the denim skirt she had put on again and flicked open the cover of the unused notebook with what she hoped was a businesslike air.

Jordan was watching her with a sardonic quirk at the corner of his mouth, his eyes cool and a little hostile.

She made a note at the top of the page, writing down his name, although she was never going to forget who was the subject of this interview. Then she said, 'Tell me how you came to the decision to leave Vancouver and come to Salutu.'

'How? Quite easily. It was winter in Canada, and I happened to meet someone who had recently come from Salutu. It sounded an ideal place for a jaded businessman, and much warmer than Vancouver.'

'Jaded?'

'I'd been working for the company for eighteen years and running it for the last twelve, since my grandfather died. I'd never known any other kind of life but the life of the company, from behind a desk, mainly. I bought and sold mines and mineral rights and shifted millions of tons of minerals and fertilisers, not with a shovel or even a ship, but with a pen—or a computer programme.

'I didn't even know that Salutu existed, except as a place on a list of the company's properties. Then a man from Salutu walked into my office and told me about his little island. And I . . . wanted to come here and see it for myself. I've been here ever since.'

'A man from Salutu? A native of the island?'

'That's right. Even Salutuans occasionally travel, you know. Quite extensively, some of them.'

Keely remembered that Tila had been to school in Australia and said hastily, 'Why did he come to see you?'

Jordan shrugged. 'He was interested in the company that mines the island—call it curiosity.'

He spoke carelessly, lounging back a little in his chair, patently at ease. Keely paused for a moment, then asked him, 'What was his name?'

'Does it matter?'

'Human interest,' Keely said. 'Names give life to a story. I can ask his permission before I use it, if you like.'

'I don't suppose he'll mind. It was Kanimea Tarabo.'

In spite of his offhand manner, Keely sensed a slight tension in him, a wariness that she had met before in interviews, nothing to put one's finger on, but enough to make her especially alert for any clue as to the reason for it.

'Kanimea?' she said. 'The young man Tila danced with at the *magiti?*'

'You danced with him, too.'

'He must have been very eloquent.'

The ghost of a grin touched Jordan's mouth, as though at a private joke. 'He was.'

'What did he say?'

Jordan shrugged. 'I don't recall everything he said. Enough to persuade me—that Salutu was worth at least a visit, as I told you.'

Keely made a note on her pad, not because she needed to, but as an excuse to lower her eyes so that he wouldn't see the hint of excitement in them. Her journalist's instinct was telling her that he was probably hiding something—maybe nothing of importance to her, but she meant to ferret it out in the end.

'It's more than a visit, isn't it?' she said. 'How long do you intend to stay?'

'I haven't decided.'

'Until you tire of it?' she suggested.

Again there was a fractional pause, as though he had to think before he answered. 'If you like,' he said.

'Surely that can't be long. Don't you miss the excitement of big business?'

His eyes hardened slightly, and she knew that she had failed to keep the sarcasm out of her voice. She would have to be more careful . . . at this stage, she didn't want to antagonise him. It might prevent her gleaning more information.

He said, 'I told you, I'd had my fill of that kind of excitement. I wanted to try something different.'

'The life of a lotus-eater? That's different, all right.'

'Yes, it is. And I like it.'

She couldn't imagine that. Just looking at him, a

superbly fit specimen of manhood—much fitter, even, than he had been back in his high-rise Vancouver office—her mind simply balked at the idea of his spending his time happily in total idleness. He was a man who needed some kind of activity, something that challenged his sharp mind, as well as his body. She remembered him helping to hump the heavy bags of phosphate aboard the barges that carried them to the ship in the bay—hard physical labour, certainly, but no effort of mind involved. And how often did he do that, anyway? The ship only called once a month.

'What do you do with your days?' she asked.

'What should a lotus-eater do? I eat, swim, laze about the beach.'

He was teasing, his eyes humorous, his voice holding a hint of laughter.

Keely let her gaze rove over him critically. 'No, you don't,' she said. 'If you spent your time lazing about, it would show by now.'

He gave her a sharp grin of acknowledgement. 'Clever girl. But it's what your readers want, isn't it? To picture a life of idyllic idleness, to imagine themselves in my place?'

Coolly, she answered, 'Not necessarily. That's the fantasy. They want to know how it compares with the reality.'

'You think so? Well, tell them it's not all that different. The sea is as warm, the sky as blue, the sands as golden as in the movies about South Sea islands. The coconuts fall off the palms and oranges and paw-paws grow wild. The waters are full of fish and the trees are full of birds. It's paradise.'

She caught a fleeting expression on his face, gone so quickly that she couldn't be sure of what it meant, but there had been an unpleasantness about it, a downward twist of his mouth, a hint of bitterness in his eyes. Her breathing quickened imperceptibly. She had a feeling that if she were clever she could get to the heart of the matter, to the thing he was trying to cover up.

But she must be careful. If he thought she was suspicious, he would clam up. Evenly, she said, 'Do you fish?'

'When the mood takes me.'

'What else do you do—when the mood takes you?'

He moved a little in his chair, stretching his long legs further, easing his back against the cushions, and she tensed a little, like a cat that has glimpsed its prey. 'I keep an eye on the phosphate digging,' he said. 'This being the agent's house, technically I'm taking his place. But the company has a very good foreman on the job—one of the islanders.'

'You humped sacks the other day,' she reminded him, with the vague sensation that something was slipping away from her.

'It keeps me trim,' he said. 'I've been known to use a pick or shovel now and then as well.'

'Do you enjoy doing labouring work?'

'I don't have to do it.'

'So it's a labour of love?'

Again she caught a glimpse of that odd, bitter expression before he drawled, 'You could call it that.'

She dropped her eyes again, doodling on her pad. 'It sounds like an ideal life,' she said. 'Are you happy?'

'What do you think?' he said, with mockery and an underlying note of something very different—something almost frightening.

Keely looked up quickly, and the expression in his eyes as he looked back at her momentarily stopped her breath in her throat. Then he suddenly got up, his face assuming a hard mask, and said, 'I'm thirsty after all. Can I get you something?'

Keely shook her head and he turned away, going to a satinwood cabinet in one corner and pouring himself a glass of neat whiskey. No ice, she thought, and almost grimaced as she watched him down it quickly, and pour again. A faint feeling of satisfaction glowed inside her, because that last probe had undoubtedly gone home. For a moment he had been thrown off balance.

He had the mask firmly in place now, coming back to the table as he sipped his drink and staring down at the little window on the top of the recorder where the tape in its casette could be seen slowly turning on its spools.

He didn't sit down again but stood, with a half-inch of liquid in the glass he held, and said, 'What else do you want to know?'

She had to feel her way carefully now. He was on the defensive, and would have to be lulled into letting down his guard again before she slipped in another thrust. 'Aren't you worried about how the firm is getting on back home?' she asked quietly. 'How they're managing without you?'

'They're getting on just fine,' he said. 'We do occasionally get mail here. The managing director is a very capable man. They don't miss me.'

'They do!' Keely said. 'Oliver said—'

She stopped at the sudden flaring of angry surprise in his eyes. He stared down at her and said, very quietly, 'I see. What did Oliver say?'

'Not much,' she said hastily. 'Just that they miss you and—he thinks it's time you came back. He doesn't really enjoy being top dog.'

'It's good for him,' Jordan said. 'He's been living in my shadow, and the shadow of my grandfather before that, for too long. All he needs is a bit more confidence in himself—and he'll get that if he's forced to make decisions without someone breathing down his neck all the time.'

She stifled a sigh of relief, thinking he had been side-tracked from the main issue, but she should have known he wouldn't let it go. 'When did you see Oliver?' he asked, his gaze suddenly sharp. 'He told you where to find me, didn't he? Why? Did he hope you could exert your charm and get me back to Vancouver to hold his hand?'

Hedging, and well aware that Oliver's parting words to her had been something very much along those lines, she said, 'Why shouldn't he tell me?'

'Because I told him not to tell *anyone* where I was, that's why. I should have made it clear, I suppose, that I meant *lady journalists* especially. Did you spin *him* that line, too?'

'Of course I told him why I wanted to see you,' she said. 'Do you know what rumours your sudden disappearance started?'

'It wasn't that sudden,' he said impatiently. 'I had everything organised to carry on smoothly when I left. What rumours?' he added, frowning.

'That you had died, for one thing,' she told him steadily. 'And that the company was covering it up because of the stock market situation. They were supposed to be afraid of the shares slipping.'

'What utter rubbish!'

'Yes,' she said flatly, looking down at the pencil clenched in her fingers.

She felt his stare, although she wasn't looking at him. In an odd voice, he said, 'And you heard the rumour?'

She looked up briefly, and then fixed her gaze on the shark's tooth showing in the open collar of his shirt. 'Among others,' she said lightly. 'There was also the theory that you'd departed for a mountain lodge with the latest lady in your life. I myself thought that that was far more likely.'

'Did you? But you decided to check up.'

'When we heard that you might have flown out to Fiji, my editor and I decided it was worth checking on. We had this book in mind, you see—'

'I see.' His voice was very dry. 'It wouldn't have bothered you, of course, if one of the more lurid versions had been true?'

'Which one?' she said, lifting her eyes to his face. 'Of course I would have been sorry if you had died.'

'Of course,' he said ironically. 'It would have done you out of one of your chapters, wouldn't it?'

She looked away and said, 'You know I didn't mean that.'

'Didn't you? You seem to have been insisting loudly

ever since you arrived here that your job is all that
matters to you.'

'It isn't *all* that matters,' she said. 'But it's important
to me.'

'More important than anything else?'

She looked at him, and his eyes were intent but
otherwise unreadable.

She said, 'No.'

He was still staring at her with that peculiar intensity,
and she met his eyes defiantly. Something passed
between them—something changed—she hadn't said
what was more important, but he knew, and he was
going to ask her to prove it. She knew that as surely
as though he had spelled it out. And she knew
that she wasn't prepared to give him that proof.
There was a lot more that *she* wanted from *him*
first.

'What's important to you?' she asked him. 'It used to
be the company, didn't it? What's your order of
importance now?'

He shifted and bent to put his glass on the table. 'I
don't have one,' he said. 'Except to live each day as it
comes—isn't that the proper philosophy for a beachcomber?'

Blast! she thought. He had retreated behind the
mask. Deciding on a frontal attack, she said, 'Some
people would assume that you're running away from
something.'

'*Some people* are welcome to their assumptions.'

Yes, she thought. *You won't excuse or explain yourself, will you?* What people said or thought had never
bothered him. He had never worried about anyone's
opionion but his own.

'Don't you have any regrets?' she asked. 'Don't you
miss the folks back home?'

'What folks? I had a few friends—none of them
relied on me. I have no family—'

'Only a broken marriage. . . .'

A muscle twitched in his jaw, and his mouth tightened ominously. He suddenly leaned over and pushed the off button of the recorder.

'Not for publication, Keely,' he said with deadly quietness. Then he slowly straightened and added, with a decided drawl, 'Now, fancy you bringing *that* up.'

'Why not?' she said. 'Is it a secret? Doesn't Tila know?'

A frown flickered between his brows. He said shortly, 'It has nothing to do with Tila. Why *did* you bring it up?'

'Professional curiosity,' she said. 'I wondered if it had anything to do with your sudden decision to emigrate to an isolated atoll in the Pacific.'

Her eyes were carefully blank as they met his dark stare.

'Professional curiosity . . .' he repeated sardonically. 'There's no end to your effrontery, is there? I ought to *beat* you!' He paused, and seemed to make an effort to control his rising temper. 'Well, I'm sorry to disappoint you, darling, but my departure from Canada had nothing to do with you—my so-called wife!'

'So-called?'

'What else would you call a woman who walked out on her husband without a word of explanation?'

'What do you mean, without a word—'

'To be accurate, leaving a brief note which informed me of the end of our marriage but gave me no reasons.'

Keely said, 'Yes, let's be accurate, please. Do you really expect me to believe you had no idea why? Women don't just walk out on happy and successful marriages without reason, you know.'

His eyes smouldered as he looked at her. 'I didn't say it was a happy and successful marriage,' he told her shortly.

'Then I suppose the ending of it came as a relief to *both* of us.'

'Well, it certainly stopped the pin-pricking, I admit,' he said. 'It took me a while to get used to peace about the place.'

'Couldn't you stand it?' she asked, with a hint of malice. 'You sound as though you missed the—*pin-pricks*—after all. Did some of them reach that calculator you call your heart? Did you have to come all this way to forget?'

For a moment he looked vicious. Then his mouth curved in contemptuous amusement. 'What are you trying to get from me? I didn't come here to hide a broken heart, if that's what you're after. That would have given you a kick, wouldn't it? You'd have liked to print it, too, I suppose. Well, it won't wash. It's a nice romantic idea, but our broken marriage wasn't the cause of my coming to Salutu. It happened before I had any idea of leaving Canada. And if you print one word about *my marriage,* I'll do a whole lot worse than merely beat you!'

Her head went up at the challenge. 'Really? You terrify me!' she said mockingly. 'What on earth could you do?'

'Plenty—believe me!' He looked so threatening that she did, but she wasn't about to show it.

'You've no need to threaten me,' she said coolly. 'If you say it's off the record, then it is.' She paused, and then recklessly added, 'Does that go for your relationship with your pretty housekeeper as well?'

The atmosphere became subtly, explosively charged, the room so still that she could hear the faint rustling of the trees outside, although the breeze was so gentle it hardly stirred them. Jordan was looking at her with a narrow, metallic stare, and with an effort she kept her green gaze as guileless as she possibly could.

'Relationship?' he repeated. 'With my . . . house-keeper?'

'Yes,' she said. 'That *is* the usual euphemism, isn't it?'

'Let's forget about euphemisms,' he said harshly. 'You're suggesting that Tila is my mistress, aren't you?'

She felt a pulse throb in her throat. She was making a

superhuman effort to appear cool and uncaring. 'Well
—isn't she?' she challenged.

'No,' he said flatly. Then, in biting tones, he went on,
'I haven't touched a woman in that way for two years.'

Her eyes widened in surprised disbelief and he gave
a harsh, angry laugh and said, 'Interview over!' and
walked swiftly, furiously, out of the room. A few
minutes later she glimpsed him striding towards the
path leading to the beach.

Keely closed her notebook with trembling fingers
and sat staring out through the open shutters for a long
time after he had disappeared into the shadow of the
trees.

Chapter Five

She eventually went up to her room and put away her notebook and the recorder. The atmosphere seemed to be stifling, even with the shutters wide and the electric ceiling-fan switched on. She lay on her bed for a while, stripped to her bra and briefs and lying on top of the sheet, but she couldn't sleep; it was too hot and her thoughts were too chaotic. After about half an hour, she got up and put on her bikini again, tied a sulu about her waist with a loose knot and opened her bedroom door. She had not heard Jordan come back, and the house seemed quiet. She left her sandals in her room and went quietly down the stairs, hesitating at the open doorway, through which she could see the path that Jordan had taken. He might still be on the beach, and she didn't feel equal to meeting him again yet. She turned and went out the side door and walked across the rough lawn towards the gleam of the waterfall, which she could glimpse through the dense green of the trees.

As she neared the trees, she saw a narrow pathway

and followed it into the cool thicket of lush tropical growth, studded with blossoms of scarlet, pink and white. A kingfisher startled her, flying a few yards ahead, in a blur of blue and cream across her vision and other birds called unseen to each other. The path led uphill, but not very steeply, and after less than ten minutes she found herself at the waterfall.

The central part was a narrow, straight ribbon of water flowing from a shallow fissure at the top of a grey stone cliff into a wide, deep pool that overflowed into a stream littered with water-worn rocks. But at each side of the fall itself the cliffs overhung the pool, and from them an intermittent flow of shining droplets dripped steadily, catching the sunlight like liquid diamonds before falling into the deep shadow cast by the cliffs and the overhanging trees by the pool and losing themselves in the dark water below.

These must be the tears of the morning, she thought, watching in fascination as the drops followed each other on their downward passage. She sat on a smooth rock at the water's edge, dangling her feet in the pool, and gradually let the serenity of the scene steal into her soul and soothe her bruised and bewildered spirit.

The afternoon drowsed away, and she pulled off her sulu and slipped into the water for a little while, floating gently and watching the tears fall from the clifftop. Then she spread her sulu in a patch of sun by the pool and lay down on it, enjoying the warmth on her closed eyelids, partly protected by the moving dapples of shade cast by nearby trees.

Someone was calling her name, and she murmured 'Jordan!' as she struggled out of the mists of sleep, her heavy eyelids reluctantly lifting as the peremptory voice came nearer. 'Jordan!' she said more loudly, and sat up, pushing tousled, sun-dried hair away from her eyes. Her face was still flushed with sleep and her eyes drowsy as he came into the little clearing, his face dark and frowning, and stopped short at the sight of her.

'Have you been *asleep?*' he demanded harshly.

'Yes.' She got to her feet and bent to pick up the sulu and replace it about her waist. 'Is that a crime?'

'You've been gone *hours!*' he said accusingly. 'It will be dark soon.'

'I'm sorry if you were worried,' she said. 'I didn't think I had to inform you of all my plans. *You* didn't tell *me* where you were off to when you disappeared from the house.'

'That's different. I know the island—you're a total stranger here.'

Somehow, that hurt. 'Is there any danger?' she asked, looking about her as though she couldn't believe that.

'Not a great deal. But I don't suppose you'd care to have a land crab investigating your pretty pink toes while you sleep. And there is the odd wild pig about, as well as some night-crawling insects which don't look too pleasant.' His eyes had gone to her feet, and his frown deepened. 'And it isn't a good idea to go barefoot.'

'The islanders do.'

'They've been doing it all their lives. Some of them walk on hot coals barefoot. That doesn't mean it's safe for you. Coral is sharp, and even Paradise had its serpent, remember.'

'Well, so far I've come to no harm,' she shrugged. 'Is that the end of the lecture?'

'So far you've been lucky, lady,' he said. 'Don't push it.'

She knew that he wasn't talking only about the natural hazards of the island. She tilted her head, her eyes defiant, and said, 'And what are you going to do about it?'

'You never learn, do you?' he said, almost under his breath. Then he moved towards her, and she held her ground against a strong urge to run—only there was nowhere in the world to run to.

As he reached for her she made a futile attempt to evade him, and the next moment she was swung up in his arms, his hands holding her so cruelly, as he turned and carried her down the path back to the house, that she was forced to give up her useless, panting struggles and lie quietly, but stiffly, in his hard-muscled arms.

The sun had gone, and the dusk was creeping in quickly through the trees. The sound of the waterfall receded, and she could hear only the twittering of the birds, gradually falling into silence, the distant whisper of the sea and the slightly harsh sound of Jordan's breathing. His jaw was grimly set, and he looked straight ahead at the path. He was holding her so tightly that one soft breast was crushed against his hard chest, but when she stirred a little in protest he growled out, 'Keep still!'

'Must you be such a beast?' she flashed at him. 'You're hurting me!'

'Where?' he said, scornfully.

She set her mouth rebelliously and finally said, 'My—my breast.'

He looked down briefly, then his mouth moved in a smile that made her shiver inwardly. 'Too bad,' he said callously, but his hold loosened just a fraction, and her body gradually became less rigid and resisting. Her hands, which had been pushing uselessly against him, relaxed, and she slid one up round his shoulder and linked them, making it easier for him to carry her. She thought his mouth softened slightly as the night blanketed them. For a few moments she closed her eyes and savoured an illusion of tenderness, a dream of what might have been—if only . . .

The house was unlit as they approached it, and she said, 'Is Tila back yet?'

He pushed open the side door and carried her into the darkness of the hall before he answered. 'I told her not to come back tonight,' he said. 'She was only sleeping in the house before because you're here.'

Keely absorbed that slowly, with all its implications. 'You mean, she was chaperoning me?' she asked incredulously. She wriggled in his arms, and Jordan put her down near the stairs.

'Sort of,' he said. 'She didn't think it was quite proper for you to be here with only two men for company. In spite of her liberal views on the question of shared rooms.'

But now, Keely realised, she was to spend the night in the house with only one man—Jordan. She remembered Tila's perturbation when she and Jordan had been conversing that morning as Keely came down the stairs. Evidently the island girl had been objecting to being told not to return tonight. But Jordan was the boss, and what he said was presumably law around here.

He moved away to switch on the light, and she blinked in the sudden glare. It also made her aware of her dishevelled hair, the crushed and grass-stained sulu and the scantiness of her attire above it. Jordan, too, seemed to be noticing, a faint, appreciative smile on his lips as he unabashedly stared at her.

'I'd better go and change,' she said, turning to flee up the stairs.

His voice floated after her, amused, almost tolerant. 'I'll have a meal ready in half an hour.'

She hadn't brought many clothes with her, preferring to travel light. She decided against the dress she had worn the first night and put on instead the silk blouse she had worn to the *magiti,* crushing down the memory of Jordan's hands slipping over its softness, of his intrusive fingers pulling at the buttons. She wished she had another blouse, but the cotton one she had worn the first day and the blue denim were both in need of a wash.

She knotted a long black and white patterned sulu about her waist and stepped into rope sandals with slightly raised wedge heels. She decided against wearing any ornament or jewellery, twisting her hair into a high knot on her head with fine loose tendrils escaping against her neck and smoothing a light gloss over her lips.

There was a light in the front room when she went down, and Jordan was lounging beside an open shutter waiting for her. When she came in and hesitated in the doorway, he gave her a grey, enigmatic glance and turned to close the shutter as he said, 'Come in. Everything's ready.'

He took a long time fastening the shutter, and Keely had the odd impression that he didn't want to look at her. She went slowly to the table and waited for him to join her.

He pulled out a chair for her and sat opposite, pushing a bowl of shrimps in curry sauce and a plate of steaming rice towards her.

'You've been busy,' she said to break the silence, which was becoming noticeable.

'I only had to heat it. Tila left mountains of food.'

'Tila is obviously a treasure,' Keely said politely.

He looked at her and said deliberately, 'I'm sure her husband thinks so.'

Keely flushed a little, unable to completely hide her surprise, but looked at him steadily. 'I wasn't being—snide,' she said.

'Then you believe me? That I'm not sleeping with her?'

'Yes,' she spoke quietly, looking down at the heap of rice she had spooned onto her plate.

'Well, that's a change,' he said.

She looked up. 'That's hardly fair. You're the one who's been calling me a liar ever since I arrived here.'

'Because I don't believe you're here just to do a job? Do you really expect me to swallow that?' He paused, watching her set face. 'You know, there have been a few pretty tourists who've come here—somehow they've heard in Suva about the islands where rich and

famous men try to get away from it all. One or two
have managed to get to Salutu, checking on the rumours and the prospects. Some of them can be remark-
ably persistent, and they come up with the most—
ingenious—stories about how they got here and why
they came.'

'You can't possibly lump *me* in with them! How can
you—?'

'I don't,' he interrupted. 'Your motives aren't nearly
as transparent—I haven't yet worked them out. But I
find your given reason for being here equally uncon-
vincing. I've found that women will say anything to get
what they want. I'm wondering what it is that *you* want,
Keely. Not just a story—'

'That's the only thing I want that I can be sure of
getting from you, Jordan,' she said, a husky note in her
voice.

'What does that mean?' he asked quietly.

Keely forked curried shrimps over her rice with great
concentration. 'Perhaps I'm not sure what I want,' she
admitted. 'I'm unsure about . . . a lot of things.'

'Well, that's quite an admission—coming from such a
liberated, assertive woman.'

Keely looked up quickly. 'Is that how I seem to you?'

'Yes. Most of the time. It's a bit of a shock. Because
you still look like—'

'Yes?' Her eyes were bright and wary.

Jordan smiled. 'Fishing? You haven't changed that
much in looks. It's—intriguing. Eat your shrimps before they get cold.'

There was little conversation as she obeyed, and over
a dessert of fresh fruit salad Jordan kept the talk to a
discussion of the island's history, sparked by a question
she put to him about the house.

'It was built by a German who started a copra
plantation here in about 1911,' he said. 'But he failed to
make a go of it and apparently returned to Germany
when war broke out in 1914. Some years after the war,

someone found phosphate here, and my grandfather's company heard of it, negotiated the purchase of the piece the German had owned and then leased the mineral rights to the entire island from the Salutuans.'

'So you don't own the island?'

'No, only a small portion of it. Disappointed?'

'No, of course not. How long does the company's lease run?'

'Fifty-five years, with right of renewal.'

'Then it must be about due to run out, surely?'

'That's right.' Jordan shot an unreadable glance at her, pushed away his empty plate, and said, 'Would you like coffee? And perhaps we'll move to the more comfortable chairs.'

He was on his feet, pulling back her chair before she had time to say yes or no. In fact, he didn't even wait for an answer, but said, 'Sit down—I'll get the coffee,' and scooped the plates up quickly before leaving the room.

Keely didn't sit down but walked thoughtfully to one of the shutters and pushed it open, leaning out to listen to the ceaseless murmuring of the waves on the beach, the occasional night calls of strange birds. Her journalistic instincts had been aroused again. Something was teasing at the back of her mind, a vague memory of something she had read, or heard, some time ago. It had been triggered by Jordan's remarks about the phosphate lease, but she couldn't quite put her finger on it. She worried at the problem for some time, but the more she tried to concentrate, the less tangible the faint chord of memory became.

A large moth flew by her, its whirring wings creating a soft breeze on her cheek and making her start. It settled on the ceiling, its wings spread, soft velvety brown with coin-sized spots of brilliant blue. Reluctantly, Keely closed the shutters to keep out any more night-flyers who might be attracted to the light from the house.

Jordan came into the room carrying two cups of steaming coffee on a tray, which he set down on one of the carved tables. He waited for her to sit down and take the one with the cream floating on top before he took a chair himself and picked up the other cup.

'You look thoughtful,' Jordan said. 'What's bothering you?'

She looked up and found his eyes on her, mockery evident in them.

'Nothing,' she answered. 'I was just trying to remember something.'

His mouth twisted oddly. 'Yes, you have trouble with your memory, don't you?'

'What do you mean?'

'Never mind. I'm not looking for a fight. It's peaceful here, let's keep it that way.'

A little nettled, Keely lifted her cup, murmuring, 'By all means.'

They finished their coffee in silence. Jordan leaned over to place his empty cup on the table, then sat back and looked at her with interest, more thoroughly than he had all evening. Something in his eyes brought a slight warmth to her cheeks, and she said hastily, 'Are you going to negotiate a renewal of the lease for the mineral rights?'

He didn't move, but she sensed a sudden alertness, and her own nerves tautened in response. 'Do you mean the company, or me personally?' he hedged.

'I mean you, on behalf of the company,' she said, groping for the answers to questions in her mind which were barely even formed. 'You're the man on the spot, aren't you?'

He shrugged and said, 'I suppose I do happen to be that, yes.'

It was just a shade too casual, she realised, and with sudden conviction she said confidently, 'But it didn't just happen, did it? All this South Pacific beachcomber business is a blind. You've come here because the lease is due for renewal, and you've an investment to protect. How much is the remaining phosphate worth? Tens of thousands? Millions?'

He hadn't moved, but his eyes were steel-grey and sharp as flints.

Keely said slowly, 'I might have known. You haven't opted out of the rat race at all! You're still King Rat, scrambling for the top of the garbage heap.'

His eyes glittered dangerously at that, but she scarcely noticed, because suddenly she had remembered the thing that had teased at the back of her mind all evening. *'Banaba!'* she gasped.

His eyelids barely flickered, and the involuntary movement of his head was almost imperceptible, but she knew she had hit home.

'What about Banaba?' he asked politely—much too politely.

'Banaba,' Keely repeated, her mind now racing, the gist of the TV programme she had seen about eighteen months ago suddenly very clear in her mind. 'It was a phosphate island, too. A British company had a ninety-nine year lease to the mining rights, for which they paid the Banabans something like fifty pounds a year. They took out—wait . . .' she closed her eyes, recalling the dry voice of the commentator, then suddenly snapped them open as the figure leaped to her mind, '—about eighty-eight million dollars worth of phosphate!' She stared at Jordan, and asked again, her voice high and strained, 'How much is Salutu's phosphate worth?'

'If the island was worked out, about a hundred million, probably.'

'Worked out? Banaba was worked out—now it's uninhabitable. The Banabans had to be relocated on an island a thousand miles from their home.' Keely breathed in sharply, appalled. 'Is that what you're going to do here? Work out the phosphate until the whole of it is stripped bare? No wonder you don't want reporters here! They might blow the lid off your plans for a new lease—that *is* why you thought it worth coming here yourself, isn't it? But why is it taking you so long?'

His face hard and angry, Jordan said, 'You've done very well so far. Why don't *you* tell *me?*'

'All right,' she said slowly, her eyes filled with angry contempt. 'I guess the islanders—some of those travelled islanders you told me about—know about Banaba, too. What's the matter? Are they being difficult? Good heavens!' she laughed suddenly. 'Have you spent half a year trying to persuade them to agree to your terms?'

'I've spent most of it trying to persuade them to trust me,' Jordan said.

Keely felt sick. She stared at him in silence, then said shakily, 'You really *are* a rat. That's utterly despicable!'

'Thanks,' he said shortly, his face grim.

Keely stood up, her eyes sparkling. 'Well, what would *you* call it?' she demanded. 'Good business, I suppose!'

'You're the one who's doing all the supposing,' he said, getting to his feet so that he seemed to loom over her, big and menacing in his anger. 'Now *supposing* you just shut up for a while—'

'*I won't!* The lease is about due for renewal, and you're getting all ready to take advantage of the Salutuans for the next fifty-five years, aren't you? Do you think I'll just stand by and let you do that?'

His laugh was brief and harsh. 'You think you can stop me?' he said contemptuously.

'I think I can have a pretty good try! It won't look so good for your precious company if I break the story to the world, will it?'

'The company can stand it,' he said indifferently. 'Anyway, by the time the ship calls here again, it'll be too late, sweetheart. The contract will be signed and sealed by then.'

'Before the ship comes back?'

He grinned unkindly at her dismay, but she recovered quickly and said, 'Then I'll talk to the islanders—some of them *are* being a bit difficult, aren't they? You almost admitted as much.'

'I did?'

'You didn't deny it.'

'I'm denying nothing. That isn't a confession of guilt.'

'*Can* you deny it?' she challenged him.

'That some of the Salutuans are being difficult over the terms of the new lease?' he said. 'No, I won't deny that.'

Triumph lit her eyes, turning to anger again as he said harshly, 'And you're not going to talk to them, Keely. I've spent months in very careful negotiations and arrangements, and I'm not having a nosy little do-gooder who knows nothing about it upset the islanders now! You'll keep out of it.'

'You can't *make* me! I—'

She broke off as he reached for her, taking her shoulders in a hard grasp as though he meant to shake her. Through gritted teeth, he said, 'Now you listen to me. I *can* stop you, and, if necessary, I will, even if I have to keep you under lock and key. What's happening here is much too important to have everything I've been working for wrecked by a spiteful little cat who's jumping to a lot of ill-founded conclusions. *I won't have it!*'

'How *like* you!' she said. 'You selfish, arrogant brute!' She thumped at him with her fists. '*Let go!* I told you not to *touch* me!'

For answer he dragged her closer, so that her hands were imprisoned and she could scarcely move. 'I already told *you,*' he said, 'I'll touch you if I want, Keely. *Any way* I want.'

Keely clenched her teeth and glared into his eyes. 'Over my dead body!'

He laughed, suddenly, and released her. 'Oh, no!' he

said. 'I like your body as it is—very much alive.' His eyes raked over her, and he said, 'Alive, and very beautiful.'

'What are you trying to do?' she asked heatedly. 'Buy me off with compliments?'

'I was trying to change the subject,' he said. 'Don't you think we've discussed business for long enough?'

'Coming from you, that's almost funny,' Keely said bitingly. 'What you mean is, I'm too close to the truth for comfort. That's why you want to change the subject!'

'No,' Jordan said quietly. 'I think that you and I have more important things to say to each other—don't we, Keely?'

The sudden change in his manner was disconcerting. She stared into his face, but found it unreadable. With an effort, she shook her head. 'I don't think,' she said, 'that anything you and I have to say to each other is more important than the welfare of a thousand Salutuans.'

'I stand corrected,' he said sardonically. 'But since the welfare of the islanders is hardly your business, supposing you leave that to me?'

'You can't be trusted with it! That's why I'm going to make it my business.'

'Oh, Keely, for heaven's sake, leave it alone!' he said with almost weary anger.

'No.'

For a few moments their eyes met in challenge, hers defiant and his impatient. Then his face softened suddenly, and he smiled, putting out a hand to fleetingly caress her cheek.

'Keely,' he said, softly, 'must we fight all the time?'

Keely moved away and his hand fell. 'I don't want to fight,' she said. 'But you can't get round me like that, either. I'm not such a fool as you think!'

'I wasn't . . .' he paused, his eyes smouldering with temper, and took a quick, exasperated breath. 'All right, then! Believe what you like—it makes no differ-

ence to me! Did you come here hoping to stir up
trouble? Is that why you won't listen to reason?'

'Reason?' Keely repeated hotly. 'You call it *reason*
when you admit that you're trying to talk the islanders
into signing away their birthright?'

'*Shut up*, will you?' he almost shouted at her, making
her eyes go wide and startled. 'I've admitted nothing of
the kind!' He stopped abruptly, to master himself, and
then he laughed, and sneered, 'Such fancy language
—where did you learn that? Journalism school?'

She ignored the jibe and said steadily, 'All right. Can
you honestly tell me you came here with nothing more
in mind than leading the life of a lotus-eater for a few
months—or years?'

For a moment he paused, and his eyes narrowed and
cooled. Then he said, 'No.'

She felt a moment's triumph, but before she could
speak again, he added quickly, 'And can *you* honestly
tell *me* that you had nothing more in mind than learning
about Salutu and its eccentric Canadian for your book?'

A trap. She wanted to say *yes*, unequivocally, but
with his grey eyes steady and hard on her face, she
couldn't. She stood mute and pale before him, her
silence convicting her.

'You can't,' he said, the quiet satisfaction in his voice
a dim reflection of the tigerish gleam in his eyes. It
almost mesmerised her, and when he stepped closer to
her she was unable to move.

'Well?' he said interrogatively, looking down at her
pale face.

'There were . . . other reasons,' she said. 'But not—'

She caught her breath as his hand came up and firmly
cupped her chin so that she could not escape the
merciless scrutiny of his eyes.

'Not . . . ?' he murmured, his eyes on her lips, his
head bending fractionally towards her.

'Not this!' she whispered imploringly. 'Please don't,
Jordan! It won't solve anything.'

His intent gaze lifted to her eyes. 'It will for me,' he

said, his voice hard. 'Two years without a woman, Keely.'

The implication of that shocked her out of her immobility. She jerked her head away from his hold, at the same time lifting a hand to push at his.

He captured her wrist, and she said, something in herself hardening too, 'Well, I didn't come here to relieve your male frustrations!'

His eyes glinting unpleasantly, he said, 'Maybe not, but you came, didn't you? You came, and you decided to stay, of your own free will. How long did you imagine I'd put up with your teasing, Keely? What did you expect? That I'd stand by and watch you flaunting yourself before me for the whole month?'

'I have *not* been *teasing!*' she protested. 'Or *flaunting myself,* in your delightful phrase!' She tugged fiercely at the wrist he still held and panted, 'Let me go!'

'When I'm good and ready,' he told her coolly.

She stopped fighting because she knew he meant it, and if she hit out at him he would still subdue her without effort and hurt her in the process. She stood rigidly still and said stiffly, 'I admit I wanted to see you—to talk to you. And now that I have, I'm quite sure that I never want to see you again as long as I live! You're nothing but a cold, callous bully, with a computer where your heart should be, and I *hate* you!'

If she had hoped to hurt him, he gave no sign that her words had found their mark. His lips parted slightly in a wolfish grin before he released her wrist, almost flinging it from him. 'Okay,' he said indifferently. 'So you hate me—it makes no odds to me. You're still a beautiful, desirable woman—my wife—and I'd be crazy if I let you leave here untouched. I *want* you.'

She clenched her hands to stop herself from trembling, and said, 'No. You can't—'

'Can't I?' he jeered at her softly. He looked at her—only looked, but it was as though he had touched her body—boldly, insultingly. 'I can,' he said. 'And when the time comes, I will.'

From dry lips, she whispered, 'Then it will be rape.'

He lifted an eyebrow and almost smiled. 'Do you think so? I've never had to resort to that yet.'

'You surprise me,' she said sarcastically. 'What did you usually do? Dazzle the poor girls with your wealth?'

'I overwhelmed them with my potent charm,' he said mockingly. 'Don't you remember?'

He advanced on her, a cruelly teasing light in his eyes, and she backed away from him, trying to edge towards the door. She had almost made it when he suddenly lunged and blocked the opening with his arm, laughing at her as she turned swiftly to face him, her cheeks flushed with anger.

'Very funny!' she snapped. Without much hope, she added, 'When you've had your laugh, perhaps you'd let me through. I'm tired of these games.'

'This is no game, Keely,' he said, almost soberly. 'But I'm not going to start chasing you around the table.' He moved his arm and said, 'You'd better go to bed.'

She stopped herself, somehow, from running up the stairs. He didn't follow her, and even after she had made a quick trip to the bathroom, there was no sign or sound of him. She hurried back into her room and hastily shut the door, fumbling for the big iron key in the lock.

It was gone. Her probing fingers found nothing, her eyes fell on an empty brass-bound lock, and she stepped back from the door with her heart pounding, her legs suddenly unsteady.

What an idiot she had been! Why hadn't she thought of hiding the key instead of leaving it for Jordan to remove at his leisure? Now he had the upper hand with a vengeance! He had let her come up alone, let her imagine she could lock herself in and be safe. But he had the key to her room, and there was no safety there. . . .

There were other rooms. She turned the handle of
the door swiftly and pulled it open. But as she stepped
out into the passageway, she heard Jordan coming up
the stairs.

There was no time—she didn't know if the other
rooms had keys and didn't even know which was his so
that she could avoid it. She stepped back and quietly
closed the door, leaning on it, holding her breath.

He reached the top of the stairs and paused there,
but then she heard him pass her door without stopping.
She stayed where she was for a while, then switched off
her light and lay, fully dressed, on the bed. She told
herself it was silly to be so nervous of him, so frightened. But she couldn't help it. And she refused to face
the real reason for her fear—the bitter knowledge that
she knew her own vulnerability. Not her physical
weakness compared to his strength, but the real and
humiliating possibility that he could make good his
boast of not having to force her. She had told him she
despised him and hated him, and her mind insisted that
he *was* hateful and despicable. But her emotions and
her wayward body kept telling her a different tale.

She lay staring into the darkness for a long time,
listening to the distant shrieks of a night-prowling bird,
the chirping of insects and the ever-present sound of
the sea. She didn't hear anything else until the key
suddenly grated into the lock and she heard it click.

She jerked upright, her breath caught in her throat,
heard a soft sound outside the door and slid off the bed,
trembling with tension.

Nothing happened, and she had a strong feeling that
he had gone away. Suspicion rose in her—incredulous
and angry. She darted to the door and pulled at the
handle, cautiously at first, and then furiously. She was
locked in.

Her first reaction was to beat on the door and
demand her release. Then caution intervened and she
lowered her hands, clenching them impotently by her
side. If she made him come to her—then what? Would

he regard that as some kind of invitation? He was capable of it. She could imagine him laughing at her anger, teasing and accusing her of calling him, and finally taking her in his arms and quieting her struggles with his kisses. . . .

Wild heat ran over her skin and suffused her entire body. Even now, her fury was mixed with a strange, unwanted excitement at the thought. She bit her lip until it hurt, bitterly angry at her own lack of self-control. If he ever guessed how she felt she was lost. He could do what he liked with her, and she wouldn't have the strength to resist him.

No, she thought. No, no! That way lay no true happiness, only a feverish, fleeting pleasure, succeeded by regret and bitterness. What she wanted from Jordan —from life—was something deeper and more lasting, something he didn't seem capable of giving. He could be kind when the mood took him, which was infrequently; he could be tender when it suited him, when— she told herself cynically—he thought it necessary to get what he happened to want at the moment. But, basically, Jordan Lang was hard all through, strong and ruthless as they came, incapable of loving in the way she wanted to be loved. *I want you,* he had said. He wanted to have her, to own her, to conquer and en-slave her. Jordan had a driving need to control and rule, not just in business, but in his personal relation-ships, too. She couldn't let her guard slip, because if she did, he would take her over, body and soul, never giving her a chance to be her own person again, but only his woman.

The thought had a certain fatal fascination; but it would never be enough for her. And how long would it be before he became bored with her and began to look elsewhere for amusement, for the challenge that was necessary to him?

She swayed on her feet and realised that she was deathly tired. Suddenly convinced that Jordan would not return, she undressed slowly and lay down on the bed, pulling the cool linen sheet over her with a worried sigh. She wasn't going to give in to him—she was fighting for her life, for her integrity as a person—and she wouldn't let him beat her. She wouldn't.

She fell asleep on the thought, and in the morning her resolve remained constant. When the key turned in the lock, she was already dressed and standing by the open window, her hair neatly pinned into place at the back of her head.

She turned at the sound of the key and waited, but Jordan didn't come into the room. After a few moments she crossed to the door and flung it open, finding the passageway empty, although a door further along was ajar. Was that his room? she wondered. Probably, but she wouldn't investigate now. Instead, she used the bathroom and then returned to her bedroom and, leaving the door open, took up her stance by the window again.

She didn't hear Jordan's step, but when his deep voice said, 'Good morning,' she turned slowly and saw him leaning casually against the door frame, one hand on the jamb and the other in the pocket of a pair of faded but well-fitted khaki pants. His shirt was a couple of shades lighter, and he hadn't bothered to button it up but merely thrust it into the waistband of his pants so that a deep vee showed his tanned chest, the white shark's tooth he wore contrasting with the curls of dark hair among which it nestled.

'Is it time for my bread and water?' she asked.

A small quirk at one corner of his mouth was the only indication that he had noted her sarcasm.

'As you're dressed,' he said evenly, 'I suppose you're ready to come down to breakfast.'

'Anything you say.'

She went towards the door and he waited until she had almost reached him before he moved aside and allowed her to walk into the passage and down the stairs. He was beside her all the way, and when they arrived at the bottom step he touched her arm to guide her to the kitchen.

'Tila won't be here yet,' he said. 'We'll get our own. Would you like it on the terrace, or shall we eat in the kitchen?'

'That's up to you, of course.'

He opened the kitchen door and stood with his hand on the knob waiting for her to pass him. Her shoulder brushed his, and her nostrils caught a whiff of sandal-wood soap blended with his own body scent as she went through the doorway.

She stood by the scrubbed table and faced him, her face expressionless, her hands limp at her sides. 'What do you want me to do?' she asked.

His glance at her was narrow and speculative. He said shortly, 'Sit down; I can fix it. Fruit all right?'

Keely shrugged and said, 'Is there a choice?'

'You can have bacon and eggs if you want. Or toast.'

'Fruit will be fine, thank you.'

He set the table, produced a bowl of fruit from the refrigerator and placed it before her, then poured juice for them both, put on some coffee to perk, and sat down opposite her. She sensed that her manner puzzled him and felt a small glow of satisfaction. This time he wasn't one jump ahead; she had him slightly, ever so slightly, off balance. He wasn't finding her easy to read.

Chapter Six

Keely wasn't really hungry, but she didn't want to give Jordan the impression that she was bothered enough to have lost her appetite. So she helped herself to a papaya.

The silence stretched until Jordan said, 'Did you sleep all right?'

'No,' she said coldly.

'I'm sorry.'

She didn't respond, and he said, 'Look, it isn't much use giving me the silent treatment.'

'I wasn't aware that I had—*sir,*' she said. 'I thought I had answered all your questions. I didn't know that prisoners were expected to make polite conversation with their jailors.'

'I'm not your jailor!' he said forcefully. 'And you know you're not a prisoner.'

'I don't know what else you can call it!' she said. 'You did lock me in my room last night, didn't you?'

'*Yes!* I didn't want you getting any melodramatic

ideas about sneaking down to the village and raising a rebellion in the middle of the night.'

'It isn't melodramatic to lock me up like a criminal?'

'It was necessary. I told you last night, I won't let you interfere.'

'Supposing I had needed to go to the bathroom last night?'

Jordan smiled faintly. 'I'm sure you would have let me know, quite loudly, if you had really needed to leave your room. I did leave my door open.'

'How considerate of you!'

He grinned again at her anger, and she checked herself. That wasn't the way to get at him, because he knew she was powerless against his strength and her outbursts only amused him.

She took a banana from the dish in front of her and Jordan got up to pour the coffee, placing a cup before her without asking and pushing an opened tin of cream towards her.

She didn't thank him, but finished the banana and then sipped the coffee in silence.

He said, 'There's a copra plantation on the other side of the island. I thought you might like to go and see it today.'

'Did you?' She made her voice sound politely indifferent.

Jordan said, 'Well?'

'What do you want me to say?' she asked coolly.

Impatiently, he said, 'Are you interested?'

'If you've decided that's where we're going today, I don't see that it matters if I'm interested or not, do you?'

His closed fist came down on the table and the plates rattled. 'Stop this, Keely!' he said savagely.

She blanked the expression from her eyes and raised them innocently to his.

He got up suddenly and she went rigid, trying not to cower in her chair. But he moved away from her to the sink, then turned to look at her, his face grim.

'Stop what?' Keely said, feeling a little safer now that half the width of the room was between them.

'You know!' he answered. 'And if you don't cut it out, I warn you, I'll do something violent.'

Her green eyes as guileless as she could make them, she said, 'I'm sorry, but this situation is new to me. I don't know how you expect me to behave. You've made it clear that I'm not a free agent, and I don't see any point in your pretending to give me choices when I don't have any. Wouldn't it be simpler just to tell me what you want me to do? I'll do it.'

'Will you?'

'I just said I don't have any choice. Do I?' she pointed out reasonably.

He looked faintly baffled, definitely suspicious. 'So you'll do whatever I say?' he asked, folding his arms before him and leaning back against the counter.

Keely shrugged, and he said, 'Okay. Come here.'

Her eyes went wide and startled for an instant before she dropped her gaze, her heart pounding wildly.

'I said, *come here!*'

He was calling her bluff. That was all it was, she told herself. She stood up slowly and moved towards him. His eyes were on her face and filled with cruel amusement. She stopped two feet from him, and he said softly, 'Closer.'

She clenched her teeth, came forward another foot and tensed as his hands came up and firmly held her, his thumbs on her flushed cheeks, his fingers pushed into her hair. He moved deliberately until their bodies touched, and she braced herself for his kiss, her mouth firmly closed and cool under his warm exploring one.

It was a slow sweet torture, and she had to make a supreme effort to hold herself unresisting and unresponsive under it. Her clenched hands were held rigidly by her sides, her lips clamped inflexibly over tight teeth.

The kiss changed quite suddenly from firm persua-

sion to deliberate brutality. His fingers tugged at her
hair as he pulled her head further back and his mouth
became hard and angry, pressing her lips against her
teeth until he bruised the soft inner lining and forcing
them at last to part under his savage onslaught.

Instinctively, she raised her hands, and when he
lifted his head at last, her closed fist connected with his
hard jaw. He shifted his grip, holding her tightly and
grabbing a handful of her hair until she had to still her
wild struggles, subsiding, panting but reluctantly
beaten, in his hard embrace.

His eyes glinted down at her and there was a tight,
satisfied smile on his mouth. 'That's better!' he said.

'Do you *want* me to hate you?' she demanded
fiercely.

'I want some honest emotion out of you,' he answered. 'Not a mask of mock submission. It doesn't suit
you.'

'You mean it doesn't suit *you!*' Keely blazed. 'You
like a fight, don't you—as long as your opponent is
weaker than you, and you can be sure of winning! One
of these days you'll meet someone up to your own
weight, and I hope I'm there to see him beat you to a
pulp!'

'Bloodthirsty, aren't you?' he grinned, releasing her
slowly, his eyes alert for any signs of retaliation. 'And
you look such a little lady, too.'

She moved away from him, automatically lifting a
finger to the inner side of her lower lip, running it over
the small sore place where her teeth had bruised. She
winced, and Jordan said roughly, 'What is it?'

She didn't answer, and he took her shoulder and
turned her to face him, teasing her lip with his thumb
until he felt her wince at the contact.

His brows drew together and his mouth thinned. 'I
didn't realise,' he said, as he drew his hand away. 'I
didn't mean to hurt you.'

'Liar!'

'Not that much,' he said curtly. 'And I *am* sorry.'

She didn't know what he expected her to say to that. Perhaps nothing, because he turned away then and began stacking the plates on the table and taking them to the sink.

Keely stood and watched. He hadn't asked for—or ordered—her help, and she wasn't going to offer it. He took no notice of her as he washed up, but she was very sure that if she made a move to leave, he would be after her like a shot. To test the theory, she took a step towards the door, and he immediately turned his head, his glance catching hers.

'I'm nearly through here,' he said. 'We'll leave pretty soon. Do you want to bring your camera?'

'Am I allowed to take photographs?'

He was picking up a cloth to dry the dishes, but he flicked a warning glance at her. 'Don't start again, Keely. We've just been through all that.'

She didn't want to go through all that again, but neither was she going to start apologising. She closed her mouth firmly and remained mute while he finished drying up. He certainly seemed handy about the house. The man was full of surprises.

He waited for her to fetch her camera and a woven palm-leaf hat she had bought in Suva. As they left the house, Tila was approaching it from the beach path, bidding them a smiling good morning.

Jordan's hand on her arm tightened in warning, and Keely wondered if he was afraid she was going to start screaming for help or make some effort to tell Tila of the danger he represented to her home and her people.

He gave her no chance, anyway, but hurried her around the corner of the house to where the Landrover was parked under a thatched awning.

The trip wasn't a long one, and Jordan probably made it in record time. Keely held her breath as the vehicle sped along the narrow road between the trees and swung around the sharp curves without any loss of momentum. There was no other motorised traffic, although they passed a couple of islanders on bicycles.

There were coconut palms growing along the coast of the island, but when they entered the plantation, the difference was apparent. Here the trees were planted in orderly rows, a measured distance between each, and even Keely could see that these trees were young, not the mature specimens she had seen along the beach.

They drove between the palms for some way before drawing up in front of a cluster of buildings. Jordan swung himself down and called a greeting to a group of smiling men who were strolling over to meet him. She thought one or two of the faces looked familiar, and from the way they spoke to her when she joined them, she deduced that she must actually have met them all on the night of the *magiti*.

The whole party escorted them down the rows of trees, explaining in a mixture of Fijian and English how the trees needed sunshine and also plenty of rain, that they were planted mainly on the coastal flat because on high slopes the nuts were difficult to gather, and that a proper harvest would not come from this plantation for another two years yet.

But one man agilely shinnied up a palm and collected a green nut, expertly sliced it open with a wicked looking broad blade, and took a smaller knife to cut out slivers of the white flesh. A drying shed had been built, and small quantities of copra had been processed there, he explained, but there was not enough yet to start shipping the finished product to Suva.

Keely could not help being interested; she photographed the nut-gathering and the deft opening of the hard fruit, and later the drying shed with its husk-fired burner, supplemented by wood until production should pick up, and more husks would be available for burning. She also took some pictures of a few cows that were allowed to wander among the trees to keep down the grass and weeds and of the horse and cart that were

used for transporting the nuts to the cutting and drying
area.

'But later we will have trucks for that,' one of her
guides explained. Another man laughed and said,
'When we have enough copra to need trucks! Don't
worry your head about that yet, Koya.'

Koya replied, 'Of course there will be enough copra!
And Jordan had promised us trucks to move it to the
sheds.'

Keely looked quickly at Jordan, but he gazed back at
her blandly and then turned to one of the men and said,
'We must be going. Tila will have a meal waiting for us.'

As he drove them back, a little more slowly, Keely
said, 'Is the plantation a company sideline?'

'No,' he said. 'The islanders run that themselves.'

'But you've promised them trucks. Is the company
donating them?'

'They're not charity.' he said.

'What then?' she asked. 'Conscience money?'

He didn't look at her, but a muscle tightened in his
jaw. 'You ask the wrong questions, Keely,' he told her
evenly.

She didn't know what he meant, but was certain he
wouldn't tell her if she asked. The closed look on his
face warned her off.

When they arrived back at the house, the table on
the terrace had been laid for two, and Tila served them
with a cold meat and salad lunch, which they ate, for
the most part, in silence. Their return had reminded
Keely of her resentment over being kept virtually a
prisoner, and Jordan appeared to be in a black mood.
Even Tila seemed to recognise that, for she cast him
several puzzled glances and seemed to be making a
special effort to appear as unobtrusive as possible.

As the island girl cleared the plates away, Keely
stood up. 'I need to do some washing,' she said, and
tensed a little at the sharp glance Jordan threw at her as
he pushed back his own chair.

Tila said quietly, 'I have washed the clothes you left on the chair in your room, Keely. You don't mind?'

Taken aback, Keely said, 'Oh . . . thank you. No, I don't mind, but I didn't expect . . .'

'It's all right.' The girl smiled. 'I'll bring them to your room later.'

She went out with the plates, and Keely and Jordan were left facing each other.

Keely said the first thing that came into her head. 'I suppose she does your washing for you, too?'

'All part of the service,' he said easily. But his eyes were keen and almost silver in the strong light.

'It's very good service. I guess you pay her well.'

'What's the matter, Keely? Still jealous?' he said.

'I am not *jealous!*' she said swiftly.

'Do you think I don't know the signs by now?' he scoffed. 'I told you, I'm not sleeping with Tila—or anyone.'

'I'm not interested!' she snapped.

'You should be. Because now that *you're* here, I intend to take full advantage of the fact—even if it's only for a month.'

'Must you be so . . . crude?' she cried angrily. 'Tila's husband must be very trusting!'

'He trusts his wife,' Jordan said. 'Trust is important in a marriage, don't you think?'

'You're not interested in what I think!' she said bitterly. 'You never have been!'

He frowned, and the expression in his eyes changed, but just then Tila came back to remove the rest of the things from the table and Jordan abruptly turned away, walking to the edge of the terrace to stare at the fragment of blue sea.

When Tila had gone, he turned an expressionless face to Keely and said in light tones, 'So, you think I'm only interested in your body. Well, it's a beautiful body. Let's go for a swim.'

Her clothes felt sticky against her skin, and the

thought of sliding into the cooling water of the sea was tempting. But she remembered the last time they had been swimming together and hesitated.

'You want to,' he said, apparently reading the longing in her face. 'Go and get your bikini.'

She took the line of least resistance and obeyed, and ten minutes later they were walking together onto the white coral sand of the beach. She was relieved to see that this time they didn't have it to themselves. Further along, a group of island children cavorted in and out of the shallows, and two men waded waist deep, arranging a long fishing net on a complicated system of poles in the water near the path to the village.

The water felt cool when they first slipped into it, but pleasantly warm when they had swum for a few minutes. Keely did her best to ignore Jordan's presence close by, although she knew he was watching her as she floated and took a few lazy strokes to carry her further out. The shouts of the playing children came over the water, punctuated now and then by a brief call from one of the fishermen.

After half an hour or so, Keely turned and made for the shore, followed by Jordan. He still wasn't letting her out of his sight, she noticed with a sharp stab of frustration.

She wound her sulu about her, sarong-fashion, and sat on the sand, towelling her hair. Jordan stood close to her, rubbing his towel over his hair and face, and she covertly watched him, her gaze travelling in reluctant fascination over his tanned, hair-darkened legs and lean hips to the shark's tooth resting on his hard brown chest, the muscular arms and the strong hands that now impatiently pushed his damp hair back from his eyes as he suddenly dropped the towel and saw her staring.

For an instant, his eyes seemed to bore into hers, sharply aware, and then he turned his head quickly aside as they were interrupted by the group of children who had been playing in the sea and were now running towards them, calling and laughing.

They surrounded Jordan, and Keely, after an instant to recover her composure, reached for the bag she had brought, which contained her camera. Jordan had gone down on one knee and had his arm about one of the small boys, and Keely realised it was the child whose cut they had treated. Jordan inspected the plaster, which was still showing pink against the dark brown skin, and gave the boy an approving pat before letting him go.

One or two of the children stared at her curiously, and she smiled at them and raised the camera, capturing their wide-eyed expressions. One of them, still looking at her, touched Jordan's hand, and he smiled and turned to the child as he spoke to it, apparently explaining something about her. She snapped the moment, the smiling man and the small, dark, doubtful child tugging at his hand.

One of the children touched her hair and then darted away, giggling, and Jordan caught him and strode down to the water's edge and tossed him in. With shouts of mirth the others followed, begging for the same treatment, and each was lifted and thrown, shrieking with glee, into the clear blue water. Keely followed with her camera, laughing with the children, who swam like dark little fish back to the sand and demanded more.

Some of them wore short sulus or cotton shorts, and there were two little girls in faded little shifts, but all were damp already and thought nothing of getting these scanty garments wet.

One of the children pulled at Jordan's arm and pointed to Keely, giggling. She saw Jordan look at her and laugh, too, but didn't understand what was happening until the other children surrounded her, grinning and calling something out to Jordan. He waded out of the water and, as she lowered the camera he took it from her and handed it to one of the bigger children, with a few stern-sounding words. She dropped her protesting hand and moved back a step as he turned laughter-filled eyes to her face.

'Oh, no!' she said, shaking her head.

'You wouldn't deprive the kids of their fun, would you?' he asked, reaching for her.

She evaded him, dodging away, and the children loved it.

'The little monsters!' she said breathlessly, but their hilarity was contagious and she couldn't help the laughter in her voice.

Jordan came after her as she ran and some of the children, deciding to be on 'her' side, ran with her, blocking his path. Suddenly it was a joyous game, and when he finally caught her she lay laughing and panting in his arms and wound her own about his neck as he carried her to the water and waded in until he was waist deep. He was smiling, too, but the smile stilled as he turned his head and looked into her eyes, and the shouts and chuckles of the children receded as a deep and wordless communion passed between them.

Then a shower of water hit them, as two impatient little boys began splashing them with practised sweeps of their small brown hands, and Jordan said, 'This is it, Keely.'

His hands tightened for an instant, and then her arms were loosened from his neck and she closed her eyes, feeling a brief, irrational panic as she left his arms and fell through the air into the cool embrace of the lagoon.

When she waded out, the children were falling about on the sand with merriment. She pulled off the soaking sulu and wrung it out at the water's edge, smiling irresistibly at their boundless enjoyment.

As Jordan joined her, she felt strangely shy, and to cover up she said casually, 'Don't they go to school?'

'Not until they're seven.' He retrieved her camera from the boy who had been carefully holding it as instructed, through all the fun, and handed it to her. 'Are you okay?' he asked her.

'Yes, of course,' she answered composedly, still avoiding his eyes. She put the strap of the camera over her shoulder and shook out the sulu.

The children were drifting off to find some other amusement, and Keely walked back to where she had left her sandals, bag and towel, Jordan falling into step beside her.

She wound the sulu about her again, damp and clinging though it was, and saw that Jordan's eyes were amused and appreciative as she stepped into her sandals and picked up her towel and bag, stowing the camera back inside.

He said, 'That looks a whole lot sexier than the bikini.'

'Can't you think of anything else?' she asked coldly.

He frowned, and she had the impression that he had stiffened. 'You make it difficult,' he said.

'I—?'

'Okay, so you don't mean to. But what did you *expect*, Keely?'

'I didn't *expect* anything at all. I was just . . . curious, that's all. I wasn't to know that you'd been . . . celibate for two years, was I?'

His eyes went silvery, coolly angry. She made to turn into the shade of the trees, taking the pathway up to the house, but he caught her arm in a painfully strong grip and said in a low voice, 'What about you, Keely? How long has it been for you?'

'What do you mean?' she demanded, twisting round to face him, her eyes indignant.

'How long, Keely?' he said. 'Two days? Did you share the captain's cabin with Sven?'

If her hands had not been full, she would surely have hit him. Her eyes blazed, and she said furiously, *'How dare you!'*

'You seemed fairly intimate,' he said hardly. 'I saw him in your room kissing you. And you didn't have much on, as I recall. Is that how you persuaded him to bring you here?'

'I booked my passage and paid for it in cash at the shipping office!' she said.

'They don't bring passengers to Salutu,' he said,

'except residents. Unless there are special circumstances.'

'Well, Michael didn't tell me that!'

'Michael? So, you're on first name terms with Michael Ward, too. What a busy little girl you've been. What, I wonder, did you tell *him?*'

She looked at the dark, angry light in his eyes, and paused before saying, 'Nothing.'

She tried to pull out of his grip, but it tightened fractionally and he said, 'What did you tell him, Keely? The truth?'

'It's none of your business!' she said frantically. 'Let me go, you beast!'

'You must have told him *something!*'

'If you want to know, I didn't need to!' she cried. 'He took me out to dinner and I wheedled him into it!' He'd believe *that,* she thought bitterly.

It seemed he did, because he suddenly released her and said, 'You *have* been a busy girl, haven't you? And what did good old Mike get in return?'

She drew in a breath, ready to tell him to go to the devil, and then she caught sight of the look in his eyes and a sudden, triumphant knowledge filled her. Deliberately, she drank in that look and laughed softly. 'Who's jealous now, Jordan?' she taunted him. And without giving him a chance to retort, she turned from him and ran up the path to the house.

He didn't follow her, and she arrived at the house out of breath and went more slowly up the stairs.

She showered the sand from her skin and hair, and afterwards spent a long time brushing the smooth tresses nearly dry, standing before the open shutters of her bedroom and looking out over the dark tropical trees and the tall palms to the distant horizon of the Pacific.

Jordan knocked once and called peremptorily, 'Are you there, Keely?'

She debated not answering, but he would come in

anyway, so she said, 'Yes,' her hand tightening on the brush in her hand, the fingers of the other automatically checking the fastening of the light robe she had donned after her shower. He went away again without coming in, and she realised he had been checking on her, making sure she hadn't sneaked out when his back was turned.

Later, she lay on the bed and dozed. She didn't want to face Jordan again just yet, and she felt very tired. She didn't know how she was going to stand a month of living under this strain. Things were not working out as she had hoped; there was too much tension, too many undercurrents and more complexities than she had ever imagined. She had not thought it would be easy, but she had expected her own reactions to be clear-cut, at least, not this confusing, hopeless mixture of misery and delight, fury and fascination, rejection and helpless desire. Of course she had known that Jordan had a powerful personality, but she hadn't realised that she would find herself struggling against him again for the right to be herself, for the preservation of her own identity. She had thought she was all grown up at last and able to hold her own with anyone—any man, even if the man was Jordan. But it wasn't true. He threatened to overwhelm her, and she couldn't allow that to happen. It *wasn't* inevitable, and it needn't happen, and this feeling that she was caught in an old, repeating nightmare had to be shaken off so that she could stand up to him and show him that she wasn't to be browbeaten or seduced into a willing state of slavery.

She slipped into a doze and Jordan was there, laughing with her against a background of snow-covered mountains and pink spring blossoms. There was a lei about his neck, pink and white and very sweetly scented; he took it off and put it on her, and kissed her, and she felt a spring of happiness bubbling deep inside her. . . .

She didn't hear the gentle tap on the door, but when

Tila came into the room, Keely woke suddenly, her
eyes startled as she came back to the reality of a dim,
warm room and the soft-footed girl who smiled apologetically at her as she placed a pile of freshly laundered
and ironed clothing at the foot of the bed.

'I'm sorry,' Tila said. 'I didn't mean to wake you. I
thought you were out.'

'That's all right.' Keely struggled up to a sitting
position, pushing her hair away from her flushed face.
'Thank you, Tila. You've done them much better than I
could have.'

'Oh, I like doing it,' Tila said. 'Jordan says I am a
very unusual woman, liking to do housework. It was
hard to convince him that I *wanted* to work for him,
keeping this old house the way it should be.'

'You *asked* for the job?' Keely said.

'Yes. I would do it for friendship, but Jordan insists
on paying me.'

'And your husband? He doesn't mind?'

'Kanimea is a very liberated man, for Salutu. He says
it is right that I should not waste my training. I have a
domestic science diploma, you see.'

'I see.'

'Yes, and there is not very much to do with a diploma
like that in a one-room *bure*, which is all we need,
Kanimea and I. So I practice my skills here and keep
Jordan comfortable at the same time. I think it is a
good arrangement, don't you?'

'Very good.' No wonder Tila wasn't treated like a
servant. She wasn't one, really. This was hardly the
usual employer-employee situation. 'What's the time?'
Keely asked, realising that she had left her wristwatch
on the dressing table.

'Soon it will be dark,' Tila answered. Keely con-
cealed a smile. She had learned already that in the
islands time was measured less precisely than in other
parts of the world. For what did it matter, really, if one
ate when one was hungry, rather than by the clock,
slept when it got dark and woke when the sun let one

sleep no longer? And in spite of her three years in Australia and her diploma, Tila was an islander still.

Keely swung her feet to the floor and moved to the dressing table to pick up a comb.

Tila said, 'I must finish preparing the dinner,' and moved towards the door.

'Are you eating with us?' Keely asked, trying to mask her anxiety.

'Oh, no. I shall go and eat with my husband. Here, a husband is the only man a woman will normally sit and eat with. It was different in Australia, of course, and I got used to Australian customs when I was there, but on Salutu . . .'

'I understand,' Keely said. 'When in Rome . . . But you had breakfast with us on Sunday.'

'I thought it was better than letting you eat alone with Jordan. But, of course, that was silly. You are not a Salutuan; it meant nothing to you. And Jordan has explained that there is no need for me to—what is the word? Chap—something?'

'Chaperone,' Keely said.

'Yes, that's right. Now I understand about you and Jordan, so I will not feel I must *chaperone* you any more.'

What exactly had Jordan said? Keely wondered. But before she could ask, he appeared in the doorway, on his mouth a tiny smile that convinced her that he had been listening to the entire conversation.

Of course he would have—he wasn't going to leave her alone with Tila if he could help it. Not with a hundred million dollars at stake if she managed to put a spoke in his business wheel.

'Tila,' he said. 'I wanted to see you about something.'

'Of course, Jordan,' she said. 'What is it?'

He waited for her to pass him in the doorway and then leaned over and pulled the door shut behind them, leaving Keely alone. She pulled the comb much more viciously than was necessary through her hair, wonder-

ing if he had really wanted to talk to Tila or if it had
been just an excuse to get her away before Keely had a
chance to influence her.

She pulled her hair back and pinned it high off her
neck for coolness. The blouse she put on seemed hot
and prickly, for the air was stiflingly warm and humid.
She pulled the blouse off and eased the band of her bra,
feeling the tiny beads of sweat between her breasts
dampen her fingers. The coolest thing she had was the
low-necked dress she had worn the first evening, when
Sven was still there; it was light and silky and needed no
bra underneath.

She looked at it longingly, and on impulse took off
the constricting undergarment and slipped the dress
over her head. If she wore no jewellery it wouldn't look
too dressy, although there was no denying that the cut
was rather daring, lovingly moulding the fullness of her
breasts, emphasising her slim waist and the curve of her
hips below. But it felt fresh and cool and when she
moved the long skirt created a welcome little stirring of
air about her bare legs.

She used a minimum of makeup to offset the seduc-
tiveness of the dress and slid her feet into sandals with
cork soles.

When she opened her door, Jordan was standing at
the top of the stairs waiting for her. She hoped that he
had been waiting a long time, but he didn't look
impatient.

She walked past him as though he weren't there. He
followed her down and, when she hesitated at the
bottom of the stairs, took her arm to lead her into the
front room.

Tila served them with her usual quiet grace and the
food was delicious, as always, but Keely hardly noticed
what she was eating. When Tila brought them coffee
and then said good night to them both, she answered
with difficulty, knowing that once they were alone the
subtle, wearing, tug-of-war between herself and Jordan
was bound to be renewed.

She sat in one of the loungers stirring her coffee, and Jordan leaned on a closed shutter and sipped at his. The tension leaped between them like tiny, invisible flashes of lightning, and she searched for a casual word that would slice through it and bring them back to some kind of normality. But anything she could think of to say seemed to be two-edged, a weapon that might be turned against her, and she finished her coffee in silence.

A sound intruded from outside, a vague whisper that suddenly turned to a muted roar, and she raised startled eyes to Jordan and said, 'What's that?'

He put down his cup and turned to open the shutters, and she saw the light reaching from the room into the darkness and dancing off a shimmering curtain of water outside the windows. 'Rain,' Jordan said. 'The rain has come.'

She said, 'Oh!' and stood up. It had seemed it would never rain here, and yet the lushness of the tropical growth on the island depended on rain, and the coconut palms wouldn't grow and produce the copra without it. She had a sudden longing to be outside, away from the stuffy room, and as though he read her thoughts, Jordan said, 'Want to go out and watch it for a while?'

She nodded, and he led her out the wide front door. They stood under the elegant, unlikely portico at the top of the steps and watched the downpour soak the ground below, falling in a straight, steady, solid stream. It had cooled the air just a little, and Keely put out her hand, collecting a little pool in her palm and getting small droplets splashed over her face and shoulders.

She drew her hand back with the rain in the hollow of her palm, and Jordan suddenly put his strong fingers under hers and dipped his head to drink the raindrops she held.

She felt the warmth of his mouth against her skin and snatched her hand away, saying in a strangled voice, *Don't!'*

In the light from the house his face looked austere and determined. 'Don't say that,' he said, and pulled her into his arms, crushing her feeble opposition with no trouble, brushing the raindrops from her shoulders with the lightest touch of his lips and then finding her protesting mouth with his.

The only sound was the steady roar of the rain all about them, and she tasted the fresh water on his lips before it was replaced by the warm taste of passion. The sound of the rain and the insistent demand of his mouth drowned all thought, and she floated for a while in a mindless sea of intoxicating, unbearable excitement.

But she wasn't quite lost yet. Her resistance was feeble, but even as her body seemed to be melting into the hardness of his she made a supreme effort and pulled away from his lips with a soft sound of denial. He didn't seem to notice it, holding her until she swayed off balance, his mouth wandering warmly over her taut throat and finding the soft swell of her breast. His hold loosened a little then, and she suddenly tore herself free and fled into the house.

Her flight must have taken him by surprise, and she was halfway up the stairs before she heard his voice hoarsely calling her. She didn't wait, but when she reached the door of her room, the room she had instinctively headed for, she stopped, because, of course, it was futile trying to hide in there. Running was futile. . . . There was nowhere to go that he couldn't follow her to, anyway. Nowhere in the world, and didn't she know that running away never solved a thing . . . ?

He had pounded up the stairs behind her and when she turned, he was standing at the top, his hand gripping the corner post. His breathing was audible, but it wasn't the stairs that had done that. He was very fit and they were nothing to him.

He didn't move, but his eyes were burningly alive, his

face pale and oddly gaunt-looking. 'Why are you so frightened?' he said. 'Why run from me?'

'I . . . don't want . . .' she stammered, whispering.

'Yes, you do,' he said. 'You *do* want! You *want*, Keely.'

She shook her head, and a faint breath of anger stirred in her because he didn't understand, and wouldn't try. 'It's too soon!' she said desperately.

'Too soon or too late,' he said. 'What's the difference? This is *now*. It isn't just me wanting you, Keely. We want each other—now.'

'And the devil take tomorrow?' she said shakily. 'No. I didn't mean this to happen, Jordan. It wasn't what I had planned—we must talk . . . don't you see?'

'Talk!' he said impatiently. 'When did that ever get us anywhere? Some things don't bear talking about, Keely. There are other ways of communicating—better ways.'

'Communicating what?' she cried bitterly. 'The mastery of man over woman?'

His hand left the stair post and he straightened. 'I'm talking about love,' he said. 'Not some kind of eternal battle of the sexes.'

Just for a moment the word made her heart leap with hope, but she battered it down with the bitterness in her mind, deliberately fanning the small flame of anger that flickered there. She couldn't afford to lose this battle, and anger was her only shield against him.

'You wouldn't know the difference,' she said. 'Love is a partnership, an equal partnership. The only kind of partnership you know is a takeover. You don't want to love me—you want to take me over, body and soul, to make me *yours*! A *thing* like all the other things you *own*. Well, I won't be owned, Jordan. I *won't!*'

'Shut up!' he said. 'You're hysterical.'

She barely stopped herself from shouting at him, screaming her denial and proving him right. 'No, I'm not,' she said very calmly. 'I'm in my right mind. I wasn't—for a little while, down there—but now I am. Yes, I wanted you then, but there are other things I want more. Self-respect, independence, to be myself, not just a sort of spare part of your life that you can pick up when you feel like it and discard when there are more interesting things to do.'

He made an impatient gesture and stepped closer to her. 'It isn't like that. I've heard all this liberationist theory before, and I've had my fill of it, Keely. I'm not going to stand here while you harangue me!'

'No, you won't listen, will you?' she flashed in fury. 'You didn't listen before and you certainly aren't going to start now! You don't allow any chinks in your male chauvinist armour, do you? I don't know why I *ever* wanted you! Or why you should have thought you wanted me! You don't want a woman; you want a computer-date robot, programmed to fill your rather *pathetic* needs. Because the truth is, you're not a *man* at all, you're nothing but a business machine! You don't have the normal human impulses that most men—'

She broke off because his face had turned to a pale mask of fury, and even as she tried to escape, he reached out and took her shoulders and shook her unmercifully.

She kicked viciously at his ankle, and, as his hold loosened, swung a fist at his face. She felt her knuckles jar against his cheekbone and her hand went numb, and then he had her wrist in an iron grasp and was forcing it down. She aimed an open-handed slap at him with her other hand, but he grabbed that, too, and from then on it was a losing battle, with her doing all the fighting and Jordan simply defending himself, holding her with hands that hurt but not hitting back. He didn't need to; he could easily win without that.

She tried to kick him again, but he moved swiftly aside, twisting the wrists he held so that she cried out in pain. Then he hauled her close to him and said in a low voice, 'Don't try that again, Keely!'

She didn't, but she strained against him, still fighting,

until she realised that the writhing motions of her lightly clothed body were exciting him. She suddenly went still and looked up into his darkened eyes.

There was still anger there, behind the unmistakable desire, and she shivered as he moved and picked her up, kicking the bedroom door shut behind them before he carried her through the moon-streaked darkness to the bed.

Chapter Seven

Keely dragged herself out of the mists of sleep and into the morning. Her dreams had been sweet, she knew, although they were fast dissipating into less than memory, leaving only a vague impression of comfort and loving and a long-term pain at last smoothed away.

She didn't want to leave her dreamland, but a strange sense of urgency was pressing on her, nagging at her consciousness. Even before she opened her eyes and saw the man standing by the open shutter, with the sunlight outlining his dark head and burnishing his bare shoulders, she had remembered and begun to shrivel inside with appalled humiliation.

He had put on his trousers, but his shirt lay on the floor by the bed, and beside it was the dress she had worn last night, crumpled into a pathetic little heap of nothing, looking even flimsier than it was.

She realised that under the creased sheet that covered her she was naked, and as memory flooded back she moaned and instinctively sat up in the bed, clutching the sheet over her breasts and putting her face down on her hunched-up knees.

He must have turned then. She heard his voice, sounding oddly muffled, saying, 'Are you all right?'

Stupid question! Of course she wasn't all right. She didn't answer him, and he came over to the bed and stood there. She couldn't hear his bare feet on the mat, and he hadn't said anything else, but she knew he was standing there looking down at the curve of her smooth back, the defeated slope of her shoulders.

Then the bed sagged a little as he sat on it, and she felt his hand softly touch her shoulder, slide across her back and move gently along her spine.

Without lifting her head she said raggedly, *'Don't touch me!'*

His hand stilled and then lifted away from her. She heard him take in a sharp breath and let it go in a sigh.

'Please, Keely—'

'Go away,' she said. 'Please—just go away!'

'I can't. Keely, look at me.'

Keely made no response, and after a moment he said, his voice harder, 'Keely, will you stop acting like a ravished virgin and *look at me!'*

His hands grasped her bare shoulders and pulled her up until her head fell back and her green eyes opened with a look of hopeless bitterness. He looked down at her white face, with the blue smudges of strain about the vivid, accusing eyes, and she saw that he had not come through the night entirely unscathed either. His cheeks looked hollow and there were deep lines about his tightly controlled mouth; in his eyes there was pain. She saw it with surprise and a faint, malicious joy. She was glad she wasn't the only one who was suffering.

'Why?' he said, his voice unsteady. 'Why won't you accept that we have so much—the rest must come right. Why are you putting up your defences again? I don't understand you, Keely!'

Her pale lips moved in a smile that held no amusement. 'No, you never have. You've never tried.'

'That isn't true!'

'Isn't it? Did you try to understand me last night? Did you try to understand why I kept saying, *I don't want this!* What did it matter to you what *I* wanted? All you cared about was getting what *you* wanted, and if *I* didn't, you'd *make* me want it. And you don't understand that *that* only made it worse for me.'

'I only wanted to love you!' he said. 'I wanted to break down the barriers between us—'

Keely gave a tiny, mirthless laugh. 'Oh, yes! That's your way. Breaking down, smashing through, *attacking!*'

'For heaven's sake, Keely! I didn't *assault* you.'

She whispered, 'No, you didn't. But there wasn't much difference.'

He suddenly let her go and stood up, his face austere. She saw that there was a line of fine, raised scratch marks on one cheek. She looked down at her arms and saw that there were red welts about her wrists and bruises on the softer flesh above her elbows.

Jordan followed her gaze, his face darkening with colour under his tan. 'All right,' he said thickly. 'So I was rough at first. As I recall, *you* were attacking *me*. But whatever you say, Keely, it wasn't rape.'

He was striding over to the door, and as he flung it open, she murmured, 'No. It wasn't rape.'

He stopped in the doorway for a moment and looked back, but she couldn't read what was in his eyes. Then he stepped through the opening and closed the door behind him with a carefully controlled click.

Keely lay back on the pillow, her arm flung over her burning eyes. What she needed, she thought listlessly, was a good cry, but no tears came. *It wasn't rape,* her mind echoed, and the blood ran under her skin, heating her body until she shuddered and moaned and turned over in the bed, trying to blot out the insistent, erotic images that danced behind her closed eyelids.

She had tried to fight him again as he lowered her to

the softness of the bed and came down on top of her, throwing a hard thigh across hers to control her legs and beating down her flailing hands in the darkness. She had fastened her fingers in his hair and heard him grunt in pain, but when he grasped her wrist, she thought he would break it and had to let go. She used her nails until he captured her hands, transferring both her wrists to one hand and tangling the other in her hair until it hurt.

Her hair had long since lost its pins and was falling about her face and across the pillow. When she finally gave up, her breath coming in long, shuddering gasps, her body aching with futile effort, he moved one of his hands, brushing the dampened strands gently away from her eyes.

Closing them, Keely gritted her teeth and choked out, 'Don't!'

His fingers brushed her cheek and continued to smooth her hair back from her hot forehead, moved to outline her ear and trail down her neck to the hollow at the base of her throat. 'Don't say *don't!*' he murmured, and his hand cupped her face and held it while his mouth touched hers, softly at first, and then with carefully controlled passion.

She lay still and tried to close her mind to what was happening, to the sweet, unwanted tide of desire that was surging through her wayward body as his tongue parted her lips and his hand moved to caress her body.

She closed her teeth, and Jordan drew back, laughing softly, and a spurt of anger gave her the strength to say, '*Stop it,* you—' but he only laughed again and put his fingers over her mouth, pressing her lower lip until it parted from the upper one. Then he kissed her again, hard and long, giving her no further chance to resist him.

She squirmed beneath him, trying to escape the insistent demands of his lips and his hard body, but every movement seemed only to bring them closer to each other, to fit her soft contours more intimately to the muscular planes of his.

His lips moved along the curve of her shoulder and back to the madly leaping pulse at her throat, and she felt his hand slide down her zipper and ease the straps of her dress away from her.

She shuddered and, moving her head in frantic denial, cried hoarsely, *'No! Jordan—please, no!'*

His head lifted then and he stopped her pleading with his mouth, with a kiss that was filled with desire and tenderness and a strange pleading of his own. Then his lips left hers and the heat and weight of his body lifted a little as he stretched out a hand and snapped on the lamp beside the bed.

Keely blinked in the sudden soft glare and looked up wide-eyed into his face. His eyes were almost black, and glittering with passion, and his tan had a darker colour under it. His hair was damp with sweat, and his face was taut, rigidly controlled. Slowly, he said, 'Okay, honey. Look at me and tell me you want me to stop now, here, and I swear I will. Only say the word.'

She stared at him, and knew he meant it, and that she had to say it then, because from then on it was going to be too late.

She fought down the hot waves of longing that were sweeping over her and closed her eyes and whispered, 'Stop, Jordan. I want you to stop.'

With a strange tenderness in his voice, he told her, 'I said *look* at me and tell me. Look at me, honey, and tell me what you want.'

It was an effort to open her eyes, and when she did, she was lost. His eyes held more than passion, and there was a small smile quirking at one corner of his mouth, and his thumb was on the pulse beat in her throat, then moving to touch her lips fleetingly as he urged, 'Come on—say it, Keely.'

A sob rose in her throat, and her hands clenched

into fists and thudded softly, twice, against his shoulders. 'Oh, Jordan!' she choked brokenly. 'Oh, please . . .'

Then everything changed. He pulled her into his arms with a strength that had nothing of cruelty in it and kissed away the tears from her fevered skin, murmured soothing love-words of comfort to her until she stopped sobbing and lay quietly against his chest, the steady beat of his heart in her ear and his hand gently stroking her hair.

She didn't know when comfort changed to something else—perhaps at the moment when he shifted until he was lying on his back, with her head still pressed against his heart, and his hand moved to her back and began stroking it with long, slow, caressing movements. Or perhaps it was not until he pulled her up next to him and met her lips with his in a gentle, almost passionless kiss. Or when he suddenly turned so that she lay beneath him, and kissed her more deeply, his hand shaping her hip bone and moving down to her thigh.

She only knew that whatever he did was what she wanted more than anything in the world at this moment, that her desire was growing and blazing into life in harmony with his, that he seemed to sense when he was leaving her behind and check himself, adjusting the pace to suit her needs. His lovemaking was the most exquisite pleasure she had ever known, and when he finally let go in the culmination of his passion it was marvellously right, because she, too, was soaring into a completely sensual no man's land where the two of them were alone together with their knowledge of each other the only joy they had ever wanted or imagined.

She had come back to earth very slowly, still locked in his arms, and had barely touched the ground when his gentle touch began to fan the still warm embers of their mutual desire, and before they knew it had happened, the embers were ablaze again, burning high and more steadily than before, so that this time was different, more deliberate, slower but with an equally overwhelming climax that left them blissfully exhausted and falling almost instantly into sleep.

If only she could have stayed in that deep, unconscious state of sleep. If only she had never wakened and realised that Jordan had so easily made good his boast, and thought how badly she had let herself down, after all, how triumphant he must be feeling now. . . .

She remembered his face as he looked down at her this morning, and a faint wonder stirred. He hadn't looked triumphant. She had thought, when she first saw him at the window, that he looked every inch the conqueror, with his proud head lifted to the sun, his feet planted apart as he surveyed his domain. And she had thought she would see laughter in his eyes when he looked at her and recalled how she had, finally, lain in his arms, whispering her desire and need to him.

But what she had seen was—pain.

There was a light tap on the door and Keely looked up in panic, hauling the sheet about her as she twisted round, prepared to call out, to send whoever it was away.

But Tila came in, a tray in her hands, even as Keely was trying to form the words on her dry lips.

'Jordan said he thought you would prefer breakfast in bed this morning,' she said. As she moved over to the bedside table, her foot caught in the folds of the discarded dress lying by the bed.

Tila looked down, and Keely felt her cheeks flame with embarrassment. Jordan hadn't bothered to pick up his shirt, and it still lay there with her dress, the two entangled now that the material had been stirred by Tila's foot.

She saw the girl's tiny, quickly hidden smile—not sly, but knowing—and Keely flinched and looked away.

The girl put the tray down on the table, pushing the lamp a little aside, and Keely almost flinched again as she remembered Jordan switching it on, watching her face as he challenged her to say no to his lovemaking.

Oh, no! Why had she lacked the willpower then? He had meant it, and she might have saved herself. Instead, she had submitted, succumbed, been an all-too-willing accomplice in her own downfall. And now he knew, of course. He knew that she wanted him, had always wanted him, would never stop wanting him, as long as she lived.

Tila was picking up the clothes from the floor, folding them carefully, and Keely wanted to say, 'Leave them; go away.' But her lips wouldn't move.

Quite matter-of-factly, Tila said, 'Shall I put Jordan's shirt in his own room?'

Keely cast a sharp glance at her, but there was nothing in her eyes that had not been there yesterday or the day before, no disapproval or embarrassment or consciousness. She nodded, and Tila said, 'Can I do anything else for you, Keely?'

'No, thank you,' Keely managed to say.

Tila laid the dress on the foot of the bed and said, 'When you are ready, Kanimea is waiting to see you.'

'Kanimea? Your husband? Why does he want to see me?'

'I don't know. Jordan asked him to come. Have your breakfast first. There's no hurry.'

There was never any hurry on Salutu. Tila went out with her slow, graceful walk, and Keely sat up, her fingers pressed against her eyes. Why should Jordan ask Tila's husband to come and see *her*, for heaven's sake? She had danced with him at the *magiti*, not knowing then that he was married to Tila, but otherwise she didn't even know the man. What was Jordan playing at?

She picked up the glass of orange juice from the tray and put it down again as sudden nausea made her clamp her teeth to fight it down. He had sent Tila to bring her breakfast, knowing very well that the evidence of their having spent the night together was obvious. Did he want to flaunt his conquest before the menfolk of the island, too?

Her sudden movement had spilled orange juice onto the tray, and she carefully mopped it up with a napkin. She was jumping to conclusions, she told herself— monstrous conclusions, at that. But he *had* sent Tila in without warning. He had deliberately arranged that humiliation, at least.

She drank the juice, hoping it would relieve the dryness of her throat, but she couldn't face anything else. She went to the bathroom and had a long shower, then dressed carefully in the crisply ironed denim blouse and skirt and hid the shadows under her eyes with makeup. She was going to look as cool and as calm—as untouched—as she possibly could. Not, if she could help it, like a girl who had spent a night of love with a man whose motives she suspected, a girl who bitterly regretted that night.

When she went down the stairs, walking slowly, Jordan came out of the front room and waited for her. She watched the stairs in front of her feet, unable to meet his eyes. Later, she would; she would force herself. But just now her feelings were too raw. She would look at him when she could do so with indifference or anger or contempt, but not now, when he might see the hurt that lay in her heart.

He didn't speak to her or touch her but gestured silently to the doorway, and she walked in and saw Kanimea smiling as he rose to greet her.

She even managed to smile back, after a fashion, and when Jordan held a chair out for her and said, with a strangely formal air, 'Would you please sit here, Keely?' she obeyed without question.

He remained standing behind her chair, and Kanimea sat down again opposite her and looked with a slightly puzzled, questioning air at Jordan.

Keely couldn't see Jordan's face, but she held herself

rigid in the chair because she knew his hands were holding the back of it and she didn't want to touch him.

She heard him say, 'Kanimea, I would like you to tell Keely, please, what I'm doing on Salutu. From the beginning.'

'The beginning?' Kanimea said. 'You mean, from when we met in Vancouver?'

'Yes,' Jordan said. 'Please.'

There was a note in his voice Keely had never heard before, but she couldn't identify it. And then Kanimea was speaking.

He spoke slowly, and with a slight accent, but his English was good and very clear. He said, 'I went to Vancouver to find Jordan Lang last year. I wanted to talk to him, and that wasn't easy, I found. There were a lot of people who were there to protect him from people like me.' He looked up and smiled at Jordan, and then went on. 'Well, I made a nuisance of myself for a few days, and finally I got through to this . . . *great* tycoon, you know? This Mr. Lang, who was so difficult to get to see. I am Salutuan—we don't get angry easily, but I'll tell you, Keely, when I got to see this man, after three, four days of trying, I was what you would call good and mad! I guess that's what Jordan thought I was, at first—a madman. I laid right into him, and told him what I thought of his company and its policies in relation to Salutu, and of the kind of organisation that spends four days passing the buck before two men can speak to each other face to face about the future of a whole people, and then I got all ready to storm out, because I knew that I had blown it, anyway, by losing my temper, when what I had meant to do was conduct a very calm, very businesslike conversation.

'Well, Salutuans, as I said, don't get angry easily, but when we are mad, we stay mad a good long time. In the old days, if you made a Salutuan angry, you were likely to get your head chopped off and maybe the rest of you eaten.

'So, here is Jordan Lang, with this big, mad Salutuan telling him his fine company is one big cheating, smash-and-grab outfit as far as I am concerned, and then I'm getting ready to storm out of the place like a very fine fellow—stupid, but a fine fellow who has told the head of the great Lang Holdings to go to someplace warmer than Vancouver, and I feel pretty pleased with myself.

'And then as I go to walk out the door, Mr. Lang suddenly is out of his chair and grabbing me by the collar and *pushing* me into a chair. And then he says, "You listen to me. *Nobody* talks to me like that. Have you got any facts to back up what you've just been saying?"'

'Facts?' A slow smile spread over Kanimea's face. 'I had a list of facts seven miles long, but I'd been in such a temper I hadn't produced *one* in the ten minutes I'd been shouting at him. So then I started talking facts, as fast as I could. At first, I didn't think he would listen, but he did. After fifteen minutes, he picked up his desk phone and cancelled his appointments for the rest of the day. And then he started ordering files sent up, checking on the facts I gave him.'

Kanimea looked up at Jordan, pausing in his story, and Jordan said quietly, 'Yes, and they checked out. Every one was correct.'

'What were they?' Keely asked, her mind racing.

'Well, when Jordan's company contracted for the mining rights—that was before his time, of course, when his grandfather was head of the company—the Salutuans didn't have any idea how much their phosphate was worth. The money that was offered for the rights, and the royalties they were to be paid, seemed like fabulous sums, just for letting the company bring in a few machines and dig a few big holes in the ground. They didn't have any idea how big the machines were, or just how big the holes might be. In those days few Salutuans had left the island, and those who did seldom returned. There were no machines here. Certainly no one thought in their wildest nightmares that it was possible to dig out the entire island, to leave practically nothing on it. We had a subsistence economy then, growing taro and raising pigs, using the coconut palm for food and housing and pounded bark from the trees to make tapa cloth for our clothes. Nobody here knew the value of money. Nobody needed it.'

'And nobody had heard of Banaba,' Keely guessed.

'That's right,' Kanimea said. 'But the world has changed. *We* have changed. Maybe that's not good, in some ways. But now our children can listen to the radio and talk to people who have travelled to Suva, to Australia, to Hawaii, even to Canada—they know there are other things besides growing taro and raising pigs, besides fishing and dividing your little plot of land among your children when you die. And some of them want to be teachers and nurses and mechanics, or doctors, or scientists.'

'Or lawyers,' Jordan interrupted, and Kanimea looked up and smiled at him again. 'Or lawyers,' he agreed. Then he looked at Keely again, and said, 'I went to Australia to study law, and there I learned about the Banabans and what had happened to them.'

'And that's when you went to see Jordan?' Keely asked.

'Not right away. I had a lot of research to do first. I studied the contract, of course, which was legal, no doubt of that. Even the option of renewal on the same terms was legal.'

Keely gasped, and said, 'That's *infamous!*'

'Yes, but it would be upheld by any court we could name. The only thing to do was confront the company with a moral obligation, show them that although the law was undoubtedly on their side, and that the islanders were bound by the contract, the company had acted unfairly and some sort of compensation was due.'

Keely stiffened and said, 'And—did the company accept this moral obligation?'

'Not immediately. Jordan told me to go away and

come back the following day. I thought, *That's that, then. He'll stave me off with some legal jargon and maybe a donation of a few hundred dollars for our education fund, or send one of his junior executives to put me off with a few platitudes about looking into the matter.* But I was wrong.' He glanced up again and said to Jordan, 'I was wrong about you quite often in those days, my friend.'

Jordan said, 'I can hardly blame you for that. People who should know me much better have been wrong about me, too.'

'I went back,' Kanimea said. 'And Jordan said he accepted that there had been a moral injustice, and—he offered to buy another island for us.'

He paused again to grin at Jordan, and, although she couldn't see Jordan's face, Keely knew that the other man had grinned back. Kanimea went on. 'Maybe that sounds fair to you. Jordan was astonished when I got mad again. He couldn't understand why one island wasn't as good as another.'

At last Jordan moved, going over to the open windows to lean on one of the supports between them, his hands in the pockets of his worn khaki pants. He was wearing a tapa cloth shirt, the first time she had seen him in island dress, the loose shirt outside his trousers. He was looking at Kanimea but talking to her. 'That was when Kanimea told me about his island,' he said. 'That was when I decided to come and see for myself. The "tears of the morning" that fall nowhere else; the special cave where Kanimea's ancestors sacrificed to the gods of war in the old times; the undersea caverns where certain fish lie waiting for the fisherman's spear; the huge old sandalwood tree that grew from the buried canoe of the island's first settlers, who came out of the sunset bearing fire and breadfruit seeds, and who were the sons of the gods; the mountain where the spirits of the ancient chiefs hold conclaves and send advice to their descendants by the howling winds, and spit words of fire when they're angry.'

Kanimea laughed in astonishment. 'Did I say all that?'

'And more besides.'

Keely said, 'What about the contract, Kanimea? Jordan told me some of the islanders are being— difficult. You want better terms than the company is offering?'

Jordan hadn't moved, but she knew that suddenly he had become very alert. She glanced at him, lifted her chin, and said, 'You did say Kanimea could tell me everything.' He had, and if he regretted it now, it was too late. She wanted to know.

But he merely said quietly, 'Yes. That's right. Only here matters get a bit involved.'

'It all has to do with island tradition,' Kanimea explained. 'We are proud people, and also, I'm afraid, we have a tradition of revenge for wrongs done to us. This makes things . . . complicated. There are two schools of thought. One says that the contract must stand, and that the company owes us nothing. Anything else, they say, is charity, and Salutuans do not accept charity. Jordan, I'm afraid, made a blunder or two when he first came in his anxiety to make reparation for his company's depredations.'

'Why don't you say to Keely what you said to me?' Jordan asked ruefully. 'That I was a typical rich *kai valagi,* shouldering the white man's burden by paying the coolies to carry it, thinking money could discharge any obligation of my conscience.'

'I'm afraid I have often been angry with you, Jordan,' Kanimea said. 'Forgive me.'

'You've tried to teach me patience,' Jordan said. 'I've never been a patient man.'

'The other faction among my people,' Kanimea continued, speaking to Keely, 'believes that the company should be made to pay—through the nose, as the saying is. They want the company to leave the island and pay over an enormous amount of compensation. They are suspicious of Jordan and his company and want nothing more to do with the phosphate mining. They say—take the money and run.'

'I don't see much wrong with that,' Keely remarked.

'Neither did I, at first,' Jordan said. 'But Kanimea had different ideas. He wasn't letting me off that lightly.'

'Lightly?' Keely said. The loss of some large part of a hundred million dollars and a huge though unspecified sum in compensation didn't sound like getting off lightly to her.

Kanimea leaned forward in his chair, his dark eyes intent. 'You see, the situation is not simple. Here, we no longer have a basic subsistence economy. The trading ships, the company store, the radio, all have an effect on our people. And the company, although it paid us a pittance compared with the profits it was making from our phosphate, has given the Salutuans money in their pockets and the beginnings of a money economy. Many of the islanders are employed by the company. Each family no longer grows its food as it used to do. There is no other industry, no cash crop, because it has not been needed. We have come to depend on the company. A sudden withdrawal would mean a social revolution. We have not prepared for that. True, we would be rich, from the compensation money. We could live on canned foods and ride around our tiny island in big cars, and wear gold watches to tell us the time of day. And when the money ran out, we would have forgotten how to plant and tend the taro, what it means to work and that money is not all a man needs to be a man.'

'But surely,' Keely said hesitantly, 'the money could be put to constructive use?'

'Into copra and sugar beet, perhaps, yes. But crops take time to mature, markets need to be developed, transport has to be available at the right time. All these things we are working on, and they will come. But the transition must be made gradually, and, when we are self-supporting, then we can stop mining the phosphate.'

'So you *need* to renew the contract,' Keely said slowly.

'In my opinion, yes, we do. But you see, the island has this very democratic way of going about things. It is our custom that the majority of the people must agree on these things before the council can act. And any money paid by the company, apart from direct wages to their workers, is divided equally. If some people spend their money on luxury goods, and others invest theirs in projects that will benefit the island's economy in the future, there will be friction. We have to get general agreement on the best course of action before the new contract can be signed. That, basically, is the problem.'

'I see. And Jordan is waiting to hear the outcome?'

'Jordan is not a man to wait on the sidelines,' Kanimea smiled. 'He has taken part in many discussions of the council, and he has used his considerable network of contacts to get some very useful people here to advise us—economists, soil scientists, crop advisors. He is acting as his company's agent, and I think he has stretched the role to its fullest capacity.'

'It gives me something to do while I'm waiting for the council to come to a decision,' Jordan said.

Kanimea's look said plainly that he didn't believe that. 'You have been of great use to us, Jordan,' he said seriously. 'And we have sometimes been less than grateful.'

'I don't want gratitude,' Jordan said curtly.

'That I know. You are what the Bible calls a just man, and justice is what we ask for. There is only the delicate matter of defining it according to the satisfaction of all parties.'

Jordan laughed. 'Sometimes I think you've set yourself an impossible task, Kanimea!'

'Oh, no! Just a rather lengthy one. And what is time, on Salutu? There is always tomorrow, and tomorrow, and the tomorrow to follow that.'

'It isn't an easy philosophy for me to learn,' Jordan complained, and Kanimea laughed.

'I know. But believe me, there are signs of progress. Trust me, my friend.'

'Signs of progress?' Jordan said. 'In the contract negotiations, or in my learning process?'

'Perhaps in both!' Kanimea stood up to clap the other man on the shoulder, his white teeth showing in the broadest smile he had flashed yet.

Keely was staring thoughtfully at the floor, and when Jordan said, 'Do you have any questions you want to ask Kanimea, Keely?' she looked up with slightly dazed eyes and shook her head.

'Thank you for coming to speak to me,' she said automatically as she saw that the islander was leaving.

'I hope I have told you all you wanted to know,' he said. 'You are a journalist, I believe—but I am sure that Jordan has told you that nothing must be printed until after the negotiations are complete? You do understand? There could be interference from outside—other companies trying to make a deal, do-gooders who think that we can't make our own decisions for the future on Salutu, professional protestors and troublemakers, perhaps. And the less scrupulous media people who would sensationalise everything.'

'I understand,' she said, suddenly realising that perhaps Jordan had had good reason for being secretive about the whole thing. What she *didn't* really understand was why he had changed his mind and decided to let Kanimea tell her exactly what was going on.

'Good,' Kanimea said. 'Jordan said he would vouch for you, that you would print nothing without our permission.'

'I won't,' she promised.

'Thank you. I'm very glad that you have come to Salutu, Mrs. Lang. Good day.'

He couldn't have seen the look on her face, for he was already turning away with Jordan, who walked with him to the big front door.

When Jordan came back, she was standing watching Kanimea striding in leisurely island fashion to the path leading down to the beach and the shortcut to the village.

She had to take a slow, deep breath before she could turn and meet his eyes, a cool challenge in hers.

His face was shuttered and expressionless, and she didn't say what was in her mind after all. Instead, she said, 'I wish you had told me what you were really doing here.'

'You weren't in a mood to listen. You were too busy jumping to the wrong conclusions. They seemed to satisfy you.'

They hadn't satisfied her; they had angered and hurt her, but she had thought that they were true. 'I'm sorry,' she said. 'I was very unfair.'

'Yes,' he said. 'Has it occurred to you that you may have been unfair in other directions, as well?'

'Are you saying I have?'

'I think so—yes.'

'But I haven't been the only one, Jordan,' she said.

'I didn't say you were,' he said. 'Last night—'

'Yes?' she said, as he broke off.

'I suppose some of what you said was true,' he said reluctantly. 'I hadn't meant it to be like that—the way it was, at first. But some things cut too close to the bone.'

'The truth sometimes hurts,' she said.

'Perhaps. But I'm not prepared to admit that everything you hurled at me last night was true. You were in something of a temper yourself.'

'I was. But I don't retract any of what I said, Jordan. I stand by every word.'

His mouth tightened. 'I'm trying to meet you half-way, Keely. But you drive a hard bargain.'

'I'm not driving any bargain,' she said. 'But that shows how your mind still works. You don't bargain with love.'

He threw an exasperated glance at her and ran a hand through his hair.

She said, 'Did you tell Kanimea that we're married?'

'Yes,' he said curtly. 'And Tila, as well. By nightfall it will be all over the island.'

'That's why you told them?' she said. 'Are you protecting my reputation?'

'Perhaps I'm protecting mine,' he said with malicious mockery. 'I've worked hard to gain the respect of the islanders, after all.'

'Would they care?' she asked.

'They're a very moral people. I think it might make a difference in their attitude.'

'Oh—is that why you haven't taken an island girl for your mistress? Wouldn't they have you? How convenient for you that *I* happened along!'

'This is why I didn't want to *talk* last night!' he said. 'It always ends in accusations and recriminations. I did not take a mistress, you nasty-minded little vixen, because I have this funny, old-fashioned, moral quirk of my own. When I make a vow before God, I tend to take it seriously, even if the other party doesn't. *Forsaking all others . . . till death us do part,* believe it or not, *means* something to me. You see, Keely, I haven't forgotten that I'm married. And unless you've got some Mexican divorce that I've never been informed of, so are you. It seems to have slipped your mind, when you were arranging to come to Salutu, telling Mike and Sven and anyone who cared to listen that you were *Miss Alexander.* I'm well aware that you went back to using your maiden name as soon as you left me two years ago. But as far as I'm concerned, you're still my wife!'

Chapter Eight

Keely turned away from him again to look at the newly washed landscape, shining and fresh looking in the wake of last night's downpour. In a low voice, she said, 'Yes. You made that abundantly clear last night—when you asserted your rights.'

The silence behind her was intense. Then he said, his voice savage, 'I wasn't *asserting my rights* last night, Keely. You must know that I never thought of it like that!'

'No, I don't. From what I know of you, Jordan, it would be quite in character.'

Again there was a short, tense silence. Then, 'Do you *really* believe that?' When she made no reply, he said roughly, 'One thing is obvious—last night was a mistake.'

She closed her eyes and clenched her teeth for an instant before she could manage to say, 'Yes.'

But it didn't matter, because he had already left the room, striding swiftly into the hall and out through the open door. When she saw him making for the beach, his back rigid with anger, she turned away, moving back into the room.

Last night was a mistake. Of course it had been—but a mistake of minor proportions compared with the disaster that was their marriage. And although she wished that the night had never happened, that she had been able to stop the tide of passion that had swept them away in the end, Jordan's sudden, bitter repudiation of the lovemaking they had shared hurt more than she had imagined possible.

She had thought he had no power to hurt her any more. She had come here hoping to exorcise the last lingering remnants of his influence and set herself free. It hadn't worked like that at all. Instead, she had found herself fighting all the way against an attraction which was as potent as ever—an attraction of which Jordan had always been aware. When they had first met she had been too young and inexperienced to hide it and had not even wanted to. And much later, he had deliberately, ruthlessly used it to stifle her attempts at independence.

She supposed that he *had* loved her, after a fashion. He had been kind to her from the start, in a casual, teasing way that had made her father smile and had roused in her an obscure feminine anger. At eighteen she had been very pretty and slightly spoiled, the only daughter of a successful machine manufacturer who had lavished all his care on her after the death of his wife four years previously.

She remembered vividly when she had first seen Jordan Lang, who was visiting New York and had been invited to a small party at the Alexanders' home. She had seen him stop in the doorway, a tall, dark-faced man who didn't look hesitant, but as though he were appraising the place and the company and filing everything away for future reference. Her father greeted him almost effusively and brought him over to her, explaining with pride that Keely had taken over her mother's duties as hostess since leaving school. Keely gave

Jordan Lang her best hostess smile and launched into
the expected small talk, trying to sound casual and
sophisticated. But when she looked up into his eyes she
saw the glimmer of amusement there. She was struck
then by two conflicting emotions: a sudden piercing
awareness of his masculine magnetism—more than
mere good looks, it was, rather, a matter of the power
of his personality—and anger because he found her an
amusing child rather than a lovely woman.

Such raw feeling was too much for her to cope with,
and she excused herself on the pretext of greeting
another guest. The next time she allowed her eyes to
stray to Jordan Lang he was talking to one of the
women, a strikingly beautiful girl of Spanish-American
descent who was a computer programmer. They
seemed to be getting on very well, and Keely was very
sure that the expression in the grey eyes now was
admiring rather than amused.

Keely didn't speak to him again until he was leaving
with the dark girl on his arm. He thanked her conven-
tionally and told her father that he was a lucky man to
have such a pretty and competent hostess in his daughter. Her father loved it, but Keely felt it was a sop, and
something of her chagrin must have shown in her face
because Jordan Lang's dark brows rose a little as she
gave him her hand and said a coolly distant good night.
His fingers tightened fractionally just before she with-
drew her hand from his grasp, and his eyes sharpened.
She saw a small movement at the corner of his mouth
and thought with humiliated dismay that he had noticed
the involuntary trembling of her fingers, the flush of
colour in her cheeks when he had touched her. It was
her first experience with sudden, inexplicable sexual
attraction, but he must be over thirty, and it wasn't the
first time a girl had reacted in this way to him. And,
worst of all, he found it funny.

She was out of her depth and floundering from the
start. She had thought she knew something about sex,
about men. She had been out with several young men,

been kissed, even been stirred once or twice. On an intellectual level, at least, she knew the difference between sexual attraction and love. Of the first, she was not entirely ignorant, though never had it happened so swiftly and so strongly before. Of love, she had little experience beyond a mild fondness for this boy or that. She knew there was more than that to real, deep, lasting love. She vaguely remembered her mother speaking of it as something worth waiting for, as something that went with marriage and should be reserved for the one man with whom a girl decided to spend her life. Her mother had been old-fashioned and very happily married. Her father had never looked at another woman since his wife had died, and he still spoke of her with love and sorrow. And he had instilled her ideals into his daughter.

Jordan was in New York for a week, and he and her father must have had a lot of business to discuss; he was at the apartment almost every evening. By the end of the week, Keely knew she was hopelessly in love with Jordan Lang. Hopelessly, because the warmest emotion she ever aroused in him was an amused indulgence.

She looked forward with a mixture of longing and anguish to his leaving again for Canada. She wanted him to be gone and yet couldn't bear the thought of his going. She supposed that she would get over this terrible, wonderful emotion then, but, in the meantime, she lingered when she took a tray of coffee and biscuits to the two men in her father's study. When her father invited him to dinner on his last night, she rushed about in a fever of preparation and spent hours deciding what to wear.

She need not have bothered for all the notice that he took of her in her sea-green silk dress with the emerald pendant that glittered at her throat. The talk over dinner was mostly of business, and since her father had never explained his business to her, she didn't understand more than half of it. When he left the room as she was pouring coffee to fetch a document from his study, Keely handed Jordan his cup and stood up to drink hers, parting the blinds so that she could stare out at the lights of Manhattan glowing in the darkness.

She sensed that Jordan had risen and come quietly across the carpet to join her. She turned to face him, her cup half empty, and said brightly, 'Have you seen Dolores today?'

'Dolores?' he repeated, looking blank.

'Dolores Montales,' she said sharply. 'You took her home the first time you were here. I thought—'

Suddenly afraid that she was making a fool of herself, she stopped. But he prompted her. 'Yes? What did you think?'

Keely shrugged. 'That you would be seeing her again.'

'Why?'

Keely flushed and looked down at the remains of her coffee. 'Because she's . . . beautiful,' she said. 'Isn't she?'

'Yes.'

Keely raised her cup and finished the coffee, turning away from him abruptly with the excuse of putting the cup down on the table.

Jordan still stood at the window, but he had turned to watch her. 'New York is full of beautiful women,' he said. 'But I've been rather busy this week with other things, Keely.'

His voice was almost gentle, as though he understood, and she didn't want that. It was too humiliating. She turned a blind, brilliant smile in his direction and said, 'Yes—with business. I wish my father would come back; the coffee will be cold.'

'He's only been gone a few minutes. What's the matter, Keely? Do I make you nervous?'

'No, of course not!' she said, making an effort to pull herself together.

'Then sit down and pour me another cup of coffee,' he suggested, smiling at her.

   She sat down again and poured the coffee in silence, carefully avoiding his gaze as she pushed it towards him. He said 'Thank you,' quietly, and she folded her hands in her lap and sat in silence, her gaze fixed on a part of the carpet where the pile was a little uneven, casting a shadow like a faint stain.

   When he put out a hand and touched hers she almost jumped, and he removed his fingers as she raised her startled eyes to his.

   'Sorry,' he said. 'I didn't mean to frighten you.'

   'You didn't.' She sounded stiff.

   He put down his cup and said, 'Where did you get your name, Keely? It's one I haven't heard before.'

   'It's Gaelic,' she told him. 'My mother had some Irish blood.' Suddenly bold, she gave him a sidelong smile and added, 'It means *beautiful one.'*

   He laughed and said, 'You're fishing, you little witch.' But his eyes softened as they returned to her flushed face, and he said quietly, 'But you are a beautiful one, Keely. The loveliest thing I've seen in years. . . .'

   She blinked with shock, and he smiled again, ruefully, but with a touch of cynicism as well. 'You know it, honey, so don't pretend I'm the first to tell you so.'

   The cynicism hurt a little, and she looked away and said, 'There haven't been that many.'

   Jordan said slowly, sounding oddly exasperated, 'No, you're very young, aren't you?'

   'Not too young . . .'

   Amusement laced his voice again as he said, 'For what?'

   She looked up, her eyes darkening in anger, and snapped, 'I'm not a child! I wish you wouldn't keep *laughing* at me!'

   She jumped up from her chair and he stood, too, putting out a hand, which she shook from her arm as she turned away. 'I'll see what's keeping my father,' she said desperately, and almost ran from the room.

   When she came back, a bare half minute later, he

turned from the window where he had been staring
broodingly at the view and went swiftly across the
carpet to her side. Her face was white and her eyes
huge and stark with terror.

'What is it? Keely?' Jordan asked sharply. 'Are you
ill?'

She shook her head and said in a rapid, strained
voice, 'I'm all right. It's my father. Please come,
Jordan—I don't know what to do!'

Her father had suffered a massive stroke. He lived
through the night and died the following day as Keely
sat by his hospital bed with her hand over his and
Jordan's fingers gripping her shoulder in a comforting
clasp.

Afterwards, Jordan took over everything that
needed to be done, and it was not until several days
after the funeral that Keely surfaced a little from the
fog of grief surrounding her and realised how much she
had been relying on him. He had asked her, that first
night, if he could contact someone for her—a relative
or friend, someone she would like to have by her. She
had said no. Her father's only sister was elderly and
unwell, living in California. Keely had never known her
well and hadn't seen her for years. Her closest friend
was a girl she had gone to school with, who was now
touring Europe. She told Jordan that her father's
secretary must be told and gave him the number of the
office. Miss Fordyce would tell his colleagues and deal
with everything there.

Jordan arranged for the woman who cleaned the
apartment to stay over for a few nights, but Keely
scarcely noticed her presence. Mrs. Holmes was a
quiet, efficient woman who kept herself to herself and
had never aspired to become the indispensable friend
and advisor to the family that the maid in television
situation comedies always was. She expressed her sym-
pathy in conventional terms, attended the funeral
dressed in drab brown with an ancient felt hat jammed

on her head and spent most of her time in the apartment ferociously cleaning everything in sight.

Jordan came every day, made her go out with him for a drive the day after the funeral and insisted on taking her to a small, quiet restaurant where he could make sure that she ate something. It was the following morning that she entered the lounge to find him handing Mrs. Holmes a cheque.

The woman thanked him and left the room in her customary quiet manner, and Jordan passed a swift glance over Keely's pale, composed face and her slight figure, clothed in a white silk blouse and a black crepe skirt. 'How are you?' he asked, taking her arm and pushing her gently into a chair.

'I'm all right. Why are you giving Mrs. Holmes money, Jordan?'

'Never mind. It's not important.'

'Yes, it is. She works for my fath—she works for me. I'll pay her.'

'I told her not to bother you. Now, don't worry about it.'

'I suppose her wages are due. I think she's paid by the week. I'm sorry, I should have thought—'

He took her hands in a strong grasp. 'Stop it, Keely!' he ordered quietly. 'You can't be expected to think of things like that just now. You've had an enormous shock, and it takes time to get over that. I'm only too glad to do what I can to help. That's what friends are for.'

It was enormously comforting, this friendship of his; she could scarcely believe that less than two weeks ago she had never met him. Suddenly realising that, she said wonderingly, 'But—I've known you such a short while. You're practically a stranger! And you've been so—so good to me!'

He stood up and moved away from her. 'Don't be silly,' he said. 'I've done what anyone would have in my position. I couldn't leave you to do it all alone.'

Realisation swamped her, then, and horrified her.

He had been unwillingly caught in a situation he couldn't get out of. She had refused all other help, and instinctively, shamelessly, leaned on him, expected him to take on the role of her sole support. She had given him no choice but to act as he had. Anything else would have seemed callous in the extreme.

She knew what she must say, but the words sounded stilted. 'I'm very grateful to you, Jordan. You've been more than kind, and I can't thank you enough. But I must start thinking for myself now, and I expect you need to get back to Canada. It's been tremendously kind of you to delay your return for so long, just for my sake.'

She stood up, thankful that her legs, although strangely wobbly, did support her.

Jordan said, 'Stop calling me *kind,* Keely. I'm not. I stayed because I wanted to. And when I go, I want to take you with me.'

The only emotion she had been able to feel these past days had been grief, acute and overwhelming. But now a stirring of the desperate love she had known before her bereavement throbbed for a second, bringing a glimmer of life to her cold heart. 'What do you mean?' she whispered.

'You can stay with my aunt—she has a place in the Fraser Valley, not far from Vancouver. It will give you a break while things are sorted out. I can't leave you—'

'But I couldn't do that! Impose on your relatives! You haven't any obligation to me, Jordan, and I've claimed enough of your time already. I'll—I'll manage.'

He thrust his hands into his pockets, frowning. Then he said, abruptly, 'How much do you know about your father's business affairs, Keely?'

'Practically nothing,' she admitted. 'But I'm sure he was quite well off. I won't be poor. I'm luckier than many girls in my situation.'

'Do you have any training—qualifications?'

She stared. 'Nothing specific. My father said there was plenty of time for that, if I wanted a career. . . .'

'Did you?'

'I—hadn't decided. I was enjoying helping my father, running our home, entertaining his friends. I had plenty to do, and I have been taking a typing course and helping him with some of his correspondence. But I haven't completed the course yet. . . .'

'He didn't tell you that he was thinking of selling out to my company?'

'Selling out? No! But what would he do then?'

'Much the same as he had been doing. He would have carried on running the business, but it would have been owned by my company. His salary would have been a high one, and the risks fewer than when he was running the show independently.'

'I see. But the sale won't go through now, will it?'

'That's up to you. The business is yours now. You can't run it, can you?'

'I wouldn't know how,' she said. 'Do you mean you still want to buy it?'

Perhaps she imagined the slight hesitation before he said, 'Yes. But the negotiations had only just begun. There's a lot of work in it yet. Books to be audited and examined, contracts to sign. Your lawyer will advise you.'

'Oh. I suppose I had better see him.'

When she did, it didn't help much. She couldn't follow the legal jargon he used, and her attention wandered frequently, the situation seemingly unreal as she told herself that her father was no longer here to cope with this kind of thing, that she was on her own. Terror threatened to overwhelm her, and when Mr. Wendell said, 'You understand, don't you?' she assured him hastily that she did, for fear of appearing quite stupid.

Jordan was there, too. He had insisted on bringing her to the lawyer's office and said he would wait for her. But she asked him to accompany her, and when the lawyer looked askance, she said, 'Mr. Lang is a friend of my father's. I want him with me.'

Afterwards, Jordan found a quiet little place where they had coffee, and she said, 'I don't know what he was saying, Jordan. I feel very stupid.'

'Never mind,' he said, covering her shaking fingers with his. 'Will you trust me to sort it all out for you?'

'Of course,' she said, lifting her eyes to his. 'But it isn't fair to ask you . . .'

'Look, honey,' he said. 'The brutal truth is that it would help me considerably. I want the sale to go through as quickly as possible, and that means your father's affairs must be wound up quickly. Would you mind if I put my own legal team on the job?'

'No,' she said. 'Of course not.'

'Good. And you'll come with me back to British Columbia and relax while all the loose ends get tied up back here. Now, don't argue any more, please. I want you under my eye. Besides, when the time comes for signing papers, you'll be right on my doorstep and it will save time.'

He took her to his aunt, whose husband ran a farm. It was spring, and the fruit trees about the old house were in blossom and the daffodils pushing through the new grass in golden bloom. She helped to cook enormous meals for the farmer and his two workers and tended the new calves in the barn. As the petals fell from the trees that burgeoned with fresh green leaves, and the calves grew big enough to go out to grass, her grief gradually healed.

She had signed all the papers that Jordan brought for her and walked with him sometimes across the springing grass to the winding river where a weak sun warmed the bark of the willows and cottonwoods on its banks. Her life seemed always to have moved in this tranquil pattern, and New York seemed very far away. Her only contact with it was through formal letters to do with her father's estate, and one slightly less formal one from one of the young men in his office, Peter Gainham. She had at one stage accepted several invitations from

Peter, and he had been at the party where she had first met Jordan Lang.

Peter wrote with obvious surprise at her having sold out and seemed hurt that she had done so without informing him of her intention. That annoyed her a little because they had not been intimate, and he was a fairly junior executive. Naturally, she had told her father's secretary and his senior man of her intention before the sale went through, but she saw no reason for Peter to feel he should have been consulted. She was surprised and angered when, on reading further, she discerned a hint or two that Jordan Lang had taken advantage of circumstances and her state of shock to take over her father's business.

She had torn up the letter and tried to forget it; rather obviously, Peter had read more into a casual relationship than had been warranted, and he was quite possibly jealous and taking petty revenge with these sly innuendos.

He had no cause for the jealousy, anyway, she thought. Jordan had been wonderfully sympathetic and considerate, but his attitude, although protective, was not that of a lover. At first she had been so numbed by her grief and shock that she had wanted nothing more, but after three months of being treated like a younger sister who needed his protection and care, she had experienced a sudden, sharp return of her earlier emotion, when she had been piqued by his lack of sexual response to her.

This time, she made no attempt to make him aware of her. Instead, she decided that the time had come for her to return to New York and stand on her own feet. One day, when he had invited her to his lovely old home overlooking the broad river with its floating islands of logs waiting to be loaded and shipped away, she told him so.

'You want to leave?' he said, turning from his contemplation of the river, his eyes sharpening into awareness.

'I can't keep taking advantage of you and your aunt and uncle,' she said. 'I have to make a life for myself sometime. I'm terribly grateful for all that you've done, but I can't lean on you for the rest of my life.'

'Why not? What are you going to do?'

'I'm not sure yet. I'll—give it some thought.'

'Give this some thought,' he said quietly. 'Marry me.'

She stared and said, 'What?'

'Marry me,' he repeated, coming to stand in front of her, a smile playing about his mouth at her stunned expression. 'You don't have to leave me, Keely. I'm asking you to be my wife.'

Incredible joy flowed through her, but something held back her first instinct to cry *yes!* For an instant she saw their relationship with great clarity—her first headlong tumbling into love, and his amused indifference; then her reliance on him after her father's death, and his compassionate, generous response; and now, when she was frightened by the necessity of being alone, of living her life apart from him, he had offered a reprieve. The temptation was almost overwhelming, but she forced herself to stop and think. He hadn't said, or given any sign, that he was in love with her. Perhaps he felt some affection for her after seeing her through the crisis of her father's death. Perhaps, in a mild way, he did love her. But he had given her no hint of any passionate feeling for her. And she felt vaguely that the love and gratitude she felt for him were not an adequate basis for marriage. And there was something else. In spite of his gentleness with her, she knew that there was a ruthless streak in Jordan, a driving determination that she had glimpsed when he spoke to her of the legal angles in disposing of her father's affairs and his purchase of the firm. It had even showed, once or twice, beneath the velvet glove, when he had persuaded her to come to Canada and made her go out with him a few times to dinner and a show in Vancouver, forced her to take an interest in life again.

She had just turned nineteen—a fact that Jordan had insisted on celebrating with one of those outings—and she was dimly aware that her life had been relatively sheltered, that she still had some growing up to do. She had been dependent on her father until he had died, and she had transferred that dependence to Jordan, like a child looking for security. But she wasn't a child, and she couldn't go on behaving like one forever. She couldn't marry Jordan because he felt she was too young and fragile to be turned loose into the big, bad world on her own.

He was looking down at her, smiling quizzically at her evident uncertainty. 'Well?' he said.

She made the hardest decision of her life and said, 'No. Thank you, Jordan, but no.'

She saw the surprise in his eyes. Then they hardened a little and he said, 'You're very cool.'

She saw that he hadn't expected to be refused, and she was faintly indignant that he had been so sure. 'I'm sorry,' she said. 'I just don't think it would be a good idea.'

She turned away from him and went to the window, staring across the water in sudden desolation. She looked at the green leaves of the trees on the steep slope to the river and recalled with vivid clarity the first time Jordan had brought her into the city, when the pink spring blossoms had lined the streets and the mountains rose clear and white-capped beyond the towering buildings in the pale golden wash of the sun.

'Why isn't it a good idea?' he asked.

Keely shrugged. 'I'm too young for you,' she said. It was a clumsy way of putting into words what she felt, but it was the best that she could do.

'You mean that I'm too old for you,' Jordan suggested.

'No,' she said. 'It's different. Perhaps I meant that I'm too young for marriage. I don't even know how old you are.'

'Not quite thirty,' he told her.

It surprised her; she had thought him older. She turned to look at him, and he smiled and said, 'Do I look so ancient?'

'No, of course not.' He just looked powerful and sure of himself, as though he knew exactly what he wanted and how to get it. It made him appear older than he was. 'It isn't your looks,' she said uncertainly. 'It's more something in your personality.'

'Is it my personality that you can't stomach?' he asked.

'You know it isn't that!' she protested. 'It's just that marriage is something that—that needs more than we could give it.'

'More than *you* can give it, you mean?'

He walked over to her and leaned his hand on the wall by the window, trapping her against the frame. She felt strangely frightened, foolishly, because there was nothing menacing in his manner, only a questioning look in his eyes. But she felt suddenly that he wouldn't take no for an answer because he wasn't used to giving in.

He said, 'What does marriage need that we can't give it, Keely?'

Her throat was dry. She swallowed, and said, 'Love, for one thing.'

'Are you telling me you don't love me?'

She couldn't answer him. It wasn't possible to lie and say she didn't, but she couldn't admit it, couldn't give voice to the strong conviction that he wasn't in love with *her,* and that if he married her without love they would both come to regret it.

She looked away, trying to avoid his keen grey glance, but he wouldn't let her. His strong fingers held her chin and turned her to face him. 'I had the impression, before you father died, that you were—not exactly indifferent to me,' he said.

He watched the colour run under her skin with

merciless eyes. She met them with an effort, and said, 'I had a teen-age crush on you, Jordan. I think you know that. But in the last three months, I've grown up a lot.'

'Yes, you have,' he said with deliberation. 'Shall we find out just how much?'

His hand tipped her face further as his other arm came about her to crush her close, and his mouth came down and caught her lips in a seeking, sensual and very adult kiss.

She made a small, brief effort to free herself, but he took no notice of that. His hand slipped to her throat and his thumb pressed gently on her madly beating pulse as his mouth intimately explored hers. She felt a hot sweet tide of desire rise inside her that she had never known before, and when his hand moved again to shape her shoulder and slide down her back, pressing her against him, she shivered with pleasure and was lost.

As if he sensed her capitulation, his hold eased a little and he lifted his mouth to make a trail of brief, scorching kisses on her throat and shoulders, pushing aside the collar of her dress with impatient fingers. When his lips returned to hers, she met them eagerly, parting her lips ardently under his arrogant demand, giving him the response he silently asked for.

'Lovely!' he muttered as his lips caressed the soft skin beneath her ear. 'You're lovely, my beautiful one. *Now* tell me that you don't love me!'

Bemused and shaken, she could only make a small, choked sound in negation, and he laughed and kissed her again with triumphant passion. Her eyes closed, she drank in the taste of his mouth, the musky male scent of his skin, the strength in the arms that held her against his body, making her thoroughly aware of his desire for her.

'You're going to marry me,' he said. 'Aren't you? Say yes.'

Instead, she murmured his name, her eyes still closed, and he suddenly shifted his grip, pushing his fingers into her hair and dragging her head back so that she opened her eyes to look into his. In that glittering gaze she saw passion and tenderness, and she parted her throbbing lips and whispered, 'Yes.'

His taut body relaxed and he pushed her head against his shoulder and held her for a long time like that. When he let her go, the tenderness was still in his eyes but the passion had receded.

They were married quietly two weeks later, and Keely moved to the lovely house overlooking the river. Jordan asked her if she would mind postponing their honeymoon and, realising that he had lost so much time looking after her and her interests, she assured him that she didn't. She didn't particularly want to go away to some strange resort, anyway. She preferred to become a part of Jordan's ordinary life, learning about him and his home.

The last part was easier. The house had been built by his grandfather, who had started the business which Jordan now ran. It was an old and gracious colonial home, surrounded by mature trees and well maintained with little change in style since its early days.

Jordan's grandfather had brought him up after Jordan's parents had been drowned together in a boating accident when their son was only four years old. Keely gradually gained the impression that the old man had been something of an autocrat, his wife the old-fashioned sort who lived in her husband's shadow and deferred to him in every way. Jordan remembered her as a gentle, patient soul and had been astonished at the depth of grief which her death, when Jordan was almost twenty, had produced in his grandfather. The old man, for the first time, had lost interest in the business, passing more and more responsibility on to his grandson, and Jordan had realised only then how much he must have loved his gentle, unassuming little wife.

The old man's saving grace, Keely decided, must have been his love for his family. The loss of his only son must have been a bitter blow. Jordan's aunt, the old man's daughter, gave her another, less pleasant slant on his character. A few bitter remarks she let slip one day implied that he had been less interested in his children and his grandson as people than as potential heirs to the business he had ruthlessly built up from nothing. 'He was determined that Lang Holdings wasn't going to die with him,' Aunt Moira said. 'He had to have a son or grandson to carry on the name. Daughters, you see, didn't count.'

But Jordan, Keely quickly realised, still had an enormous respect and love for his grandfather's memory. He regarded Lang Holdings as almost a sacred trust, she sometimes thought. The company was his life, and he was its lifeblood, for he made the decisions, just as his grandfather had. When she went to the huge building that housed its offices and was shown about by one of Jordan's employees, because he was too tied up to conduct her on the guided tour himself, there were several old hands who remembered 'Old Man Lang' and were eager to tell her how much his grandson resembled him in character.

Keely didn't want to believe that. To her, he was unfailingly considerate and tender. He made love to her with a single-minded passion which she soon learned to match, and that completely dispelled the fear that he thought of her as a child. Anything she wanted was provided for her immediately, and when he discovered her interest in photography, a hobby which she had pursued since her father had presented her with a camera on her twelfth birthday, he had a room converted into a well-equipped darkroom for her. She stifled the thought that he had done it to still her mild protests about the amount of time she spent alone while he worked long hours at the office; instead, she thanked him sweetly and sincerely and spent a lot of time going about in the car he had bought for her and photographing the magnificent scenery of British Columbia.

She fitted easily into the role of hostess when he

entertained and glowed when he praised her for the organisation of their parties. She was very happy; Jordan was an ideal husband—even when she confessed with trepidation that she had run the car into a tree, he was only concerned with her safety and laughed when she told him there would be an enormous repair bill.

Then one day she had an unexpected visitor, a nervous little middle-aged woman whom she vaguely remembered as having been present at a dinner party for senior staff, along with her husband.

'Yes, of course I remember you, Mrs. Hudson,' she assured the woman, who had expressed her doubt on that point. 'And your husband—he's a bird fancier, isn't he?' She had exchanged a few words with him on bird photography, and fortunately he had stuck in her mind.

'Yes,' Mrs. Hudson said, her worried face brightening a little as she sat uneasily on the very edge of the comfortable armchair Keely had indicated for her. 'It's—it's about my husband. He—he's lost his job, you see. They said his services are no longer required, and it's so difficult to get another job at his age—only eight years to go to retirement. I shouldn't ask you, but I can't think of anything else to do. Mrs. Lang, couldn't you talk to Mr. Lang? Al's worked for the company all his life! It doesn't seem fair! '

It didn't seem fair, Keely agreed, when she heard the story that the distressed woman had come to tell her. She assured her she would do what she could, and that evening she tackled Jordan about it. She had thought he might be slightly irritated, but she was unprepared for white-faced fury.

'She came *here?*' he said. 'For heaven's sake, Keely, why didn't you refuse to see her?'

'Why on earth should I?' Keely said. 'She's been a guest in our home—her husband works for you! Or he did, until you sacked him in what seems to have been a particularly callous way!'

Angrily, Jordan said, 'I did no sacking. It was the

department manager's decision, and I won't interfere with it.'

'Jordan, I promised Mrs. Hudson—'

'You had *no right* to promise anything on my behalf,' he said coldly. 'I won't have you involving yourself in company affairs, Keely!'

'I want to share your life,' she said, her voice trembling. 'Sometimes I think the company is your life.'

'You're a different part of my life,' he said, his voice softening. 'A precious one. It's a jungle out there, and I want you untainted by all that. Coming home is like finding an oasis in the desert. You refresh me. When I come to you, I want to leave the company behind, not find its problems waiting on my doorstep.'

He took her in his arms and, resting against him, she said, 'I thought you enjoyed it all, the challenge of business.'

'I never thought about it. I suppose I do, but one doesn't want to be challenged all the time. I need a respite from that—I need you.'

Dimly, she understood and was glad of and touched by his confession of need. She reached up and kissed him. 'I'm sorry,' she said. 'But poor Mrs. Hudson was so worried for her husband, and, after all, I have a husband, too.'

But he was scarcely listening. When her lips left his he began pressing small kisses along her brow, and as she finished speaking his lips moved along her cheek and touched the faint hollow beneath her ear. Tiny shivers of pleasure chased each other up and down her spine, and as he made to loosen her, reluctantly muttering something about dinner, she moved her head and gave her mouth to him.

When at last he freed her from his dizzying, satisfying kiss, she said teasingly, 'What about dinner?' But her hands caressed his neck, and she pressed herself softly against him.

'Forget it,' he growled, and swung her up in his arms to carry her to their bedroom.

Some time later, as she lay with her cheek against his chest and his hand idly stroking her hair, she said, 'Jordan—isn't there something you can do for the Hudsons? You're the boss, after all. He wasn't dishonest, he just couldn't quite cope with the new methods. Could you perhaps find him something less demanding?'

The hand on her hair stilled. 'For your sake?' Jordan asked, his voice sounding odd.

'Yes,' she said. 'For my sake.'

Then she cried out sharply as his fingers closed on her hair and turned her until she lay beneath him, her eyes wide with shock and pain.

'Don't *ever* do that to me again!' he grated.

'*Do what?*' she cried, bewildered and frightened. 'Jordan, you're hurting me!'

'Ask me for favours in return for sex,' he explained brutally. 'I want you to love me, not sell yourself to me—and next time you try that trick, I'll *really* hurt you!'

Chapter Nine

That had been the beginning of the end, Keely told herself bleakly as she wandered restlessly back to the window and looked out at the peaceful, sun-washed, tropical scene. The rain seemed to have intensified the scents of the flowers, and a spicy, sweet mixture of fragrances was borne into the room on a soft, warm breeze; ginger and frangipani, sandalwood and jasmine, and the faint, salty tang of the sea. But her mind was far away. . . .

She had been scrupulous, after that, in avoiding any mention of the company's affairs. If Jordan ever spoke of the company to her, it was in the most general terms, and her answers were noncommittal because she was afraid to rouse his anger again. And the accusation that she had used sex to obtain favours hurt her so deeply that it put a constraint on the sweet aftermath of all their lovemaking. She felt a curb on the spontaneous outpourings that had once naturally followed the deep intimacy of their bodies, and gradually they ceased talking altogether at those times. Jordan seemed not to miss those drowsy, murmured conversations, but Keely felt that something precious had been lost.

Soon afterwards, a friend of Jordan's had admired some of her photographs that she had hung in the entrance hall of the house. He was in advertising and had an eye for colour and composition.

'These are good!' he said. 'Professional standard, in fact. Have you sold any of your work?'

Jordan said, 'Keely does it for pleasure, Jack. She's an amateur, and a good one.'

He spoke with lazy pride, but somehow the 'amateur' label, although perfectly true, rankled with Keely. Jack had planted the germ of an idea, and when Keely took a series of pictures of a neighbour's child playing with a new puppy she captioned the prints and sent them to a national women's magazine.

When they were accepted for publication she felt a thrill of achievement such as she had never experienced before. Jordan's reaction was somehow disappointing. He congratulated her, grinned and called her a clever girl. It was all she could have expected, and yet she wasn't satisfied. She showed him the pictures when they were printed in the magazine, and he put his arm around her and leafed casually through the pages and said they looked good. She felt like a child who had been patted on the head for doing well at school and had to swallow an obscure, illogical anger.

She sold a few more photo essays and some single prints, and then she took a commission to produce a set of landscapes for a calendar. She spent a lot of time on it, and when it was finished Jordan said, 'Well, thank heaven that's over. I don't expect you to take any more commissions, Keely.'

Something hot and alien rose inside her. 'What do you mean?' she said, her voice sounding odd in her own ears.

He looked at her with surprise, and said, 'You heard

me. It takes too much out of you. You've been in that wretched darkroom until all hours these last few nights. I won't have you tiring yourself like this again.'

Perhaps if she had not been so tired she might have replied differently. As it was, she snapped, 'Don't be so bossy! If I want to take commissions I'll take them, and you can't stop me!'

There followed a blazing row, the first of many that had taken place over what Keely increasingly came to think of as her work. Because there *were* more commissions, and she insisted on her right to take them. It was a symbol of her struggle for independence from Jordan's dominating personality. She didn't make a great deal of money, and most of the work offered her was through friends. Sometimes she wondered why Jordan didn't tell them outright that he didn't want them giving commissions to his wife; she concluded that he was too proud to let any outsider know of their differences.

Sometimes the arguments ended with Jordan leaving the house in a white-faced fury. Sometimes Keely stormed off to the bedroom, sobbing with angry frustration. And sometimes they culminated in a physical confrontation, Jordan gripping her shoulders to shake her and Keely beating her closed fists against his chest until the flame of anger changed to a flame of passion and he hauled her into his arms and kissed her into a temporary, helpless submission that soon flared into desire.

They had been married for eighteen months when Keely discovered she was pregnant. She kept the knowledge to herself, not certain how Jordan would react. He had at first insisted that they shouldn't start a family right away, but in one of his bitter moods he had said harshly that what she needed was a baby to occupy her time. And she had shouted at him, 'What a typically male chauvinist attitude! There are other things in life than having babies, you know! You'd like to see me tied down to the house with half a dozen children clinging to my skirts, wouldn't you?'

He laughed unkindly and said, 'I doubt if you could cope with one—you're nothing but a spoilt child yourself!'

'If I am, it's because you try to keep me that way!' she cried passionately. 'You just don't want me to have a life of my own!'

'You said once that you wanted to share mine.'

'I did! But you won't let me! You're sufficient unto yourself, Jordan.'

'But not sufficient for you, it seems.'

'You don't understand!' she said tiredly, depressed by her inability to put into words what she felt. 'It isn't enough just to be your wife. I have to be myself, as well.'

'Am I stopping you?'

'You're having a pretty good try!' she accused him.

He regarded her in frowning silence, his mouth set in a grim line. Then he said, 'Okay. Do what you like. I won't stand in your way.'

She was so stunned by his capitulation that she couldn't speak. And, abruptly, he had turned away and left the room.

He made absolutely no further comment on her attempts to make a career for herself. But to her dismay he seemed to have erected an invisible wall between them. He treated her almost as though he was a polite, casual acquaintance, mildly interested in her doings and her welfare. Except on the nights when he turned to her in the darkness and made silent, absorbed love to her with an almost ferocious delight in her body. But in the morning, the wall would be there again, and nothing she did seemed able to penetrate it.

So when she could hide her condition no longer, and she knew that soon—very soon—his seeking hands would find and interpret the changes that were taking place in her body, she told him, baldly and in flat tones to hide her anxiety about his feelings, that she was going to have a baby.

He had just come home from the office and was

pouring drinks for them both. He had handed her a glass and was mixing a drink for himself with his back to her. She saw his hands still for a moment, and then he finished what he was doing and turned to face her, his expression closed.

'Are you sure?' he said.

'I've been sure for weeks,' she told him.

He shot a quick, unreadable glance at her, and his jaw seemed to tighten. 'Were you thinking of getting rid of it?' he asked harshly.

The thought had never crossed her mind, and the question came like a body blow. '*No!*' she gasped. 'Why should you think that?'

'You've taken a mighty long time to let me in on it, haven't you?'

'I wasn't sure how you would take it,' she said in a low voice, putting down her glass because her hand was shaking and she couldn't face the thought of drinking the stuff, anyway.

'How did you *expect* me to take it?' he asked roughly.

And Keely turned a stricken face to him, and said, 'Not—not like this.'

She felt the hot tears behind her eyes and fled from him.

He found her lying on the bed and sobbing into the pillow. When she felt his weight beside her as he sat down and placed a hand on her shoulder, she caught her breath for an instant and tried to gulp down the tears.

She resisted his hands, but he turned her and pulled her up against him and held her against his shoulder, his voice husky as he murmured into her hair, 'Don't, honey—please! Don't cry.'

When at last she lay exhausted and quiet in his embrace, he said softly, 'Keely—tell me something. How did you feel when you first knew?'

'Happy,' she said, her voice muffled against his shirt. 'It was so marvellous.'

His arms tightened about her, and he said. 'Yes, it is.

That's how I felt, too, when you told me. But I was afraid you didn't want it. That you would feel it interfered with your plans.'

'What plans?'

'Your plans for a career.'

'Oh. It needn't. Lots of women have a family and a job, these days. It's mainly a matter of organisation.'

She felt him stiffen, and his arms fell away as he stood up. 'Yes, I suppose so,' he said in clipped tones. 'No doubt you have it all worked out.'

'Not yet.' She put out a hand to him, pleadingly. 'Jordan?'

For a moment she thought he was going to ignore the gesture. Then his fingers curled tightly about hers.

She said, 'I'm sorry I didn't tell you before. We've been so—apart lately that I wasn't sure how you would feel about it.' She meant that she wasn't sure if he still cared for her. She wanted reassurance.

He said, 'I want this child, Keely. Very much.' His fingers tightened on her hand and he suddenly raised it to his lips and pressed a kiss on her wrist.

Then, as though the gesture had embarrassed him, he released her abruptly, and, saying, 'Get some rest,' he left her alone.

He seemed to make an effort after that to spend more time with her, and, perhaps because he insisted on treating her as if she were made of glass she began to feel slightly suffocated. She couldn't shake off the nagging knowledge that Jordan's assurance that he wanted the child had held little comfort for her. It should have been a joyful fulfillment of their love for each other, but she kept morbidly recalling his remark that a baby would occupy her time, with its implication that it would tie her into settling down into being the kind of wife he evidently wanted. There were times when she resented the bouts of morning sickness and the lethargy that accompanied the early part of her pregnancy, when her sense of joyous hope was swamped by dismay as she watched her figure change its slim outline and wondered if Jordan was repulsed by it. He made love to her rarely, in the dark, and with a new restraint that might have been consideration—or a waning of passion.

She took the car one day, stowing her camera and a packed lunch in the glove box, and drove for miles into the mountains and beyond the snow line, where the air was sharp and cold and the sunlight glittered on crystals of ice clinging to the dark pines.

Taking her camera, she walked among the trees, her boots crunching on the crispness of the snow, and stopped to take pictures of the mountains with their jagged grey peaks thrusting through the snowcaps, framed by snow-laden branches, and of the tiny icicles threaded along a bare twig like glittering jewels on a necklace.

She clambered into the branches of a tree to get the right angle for a shot of a frozen waterfall, reduced to a narrow trickle in the centre of a cascade of blue-tinged ice. It wasn't until the branch broke beneath her and she found her camera slipping from her grasp as she clutched frantically and found nothing to break her fall that she remembered, with wrenching horror, that she carried another life within her, for which she was responsible.

She knew that Jordan blamed her for the loss of the baby. He never said so, but it was in his remote, shuttered expression when he looked at her, and in the impersonal consideration with which he treated her after her return from the hospital.

They never discussed it; in fact, they discussed nothing, it seemed, except the merest trivialities. It sometimes frightened her that they had no real conversations anymore, but most of the time she was wrapped in a grey fog of numbness where nothing mattered a great deal. Even when she entered her darkroom one day and emerged, vaguely puzzled, with the remains of her smashed camera in her hand and found Jordan watching her with a strange expression on his dark face, she couldn't feel anything.

She said, 'It's odd. I don't remember breaking it. After I fell, I remember picking it up and taking it back to the car. I didn't realise it was broken.'

'It wasn't—then,' he said curtly, and she stared stupidly for a long time before she realised what he was telling her. 'I'll buy you another,' he said.

She stood quite still for several minutes after he had gone away, her heart beating with dull, heavy thuds. She looked at the wreckage in her hand and realised that of course it hadn't been caused by a simple fall. Jordan had such iron control over his emotions—and yet he had wreaked this thorough, furious destruction. The thought was frightening.

She returned to the darkroom and placed the camera on the bench. It was the last time she went in there, and when Jordan gave her a new camera she didn't even open the box, just thanked him mechanically and hid the box at the back of a large, seldom-used cupboard.

When she had recovered physically she made an effort to take up the threads of normal life again. It was she who insisted on giving a dinner party, who asked Jordan to obtain tickets for a new show. She forced herself to smile again and be gay and fought down a bitter anger when Jordan appeared pleased with her, when he smiled at her with approval and kissed her cheek.

She denied him her lips. And her bed. There was a bleak satisfaction in that. His touch left her cold and uncaring, and she was glad that his power to make her respond to him, even against her will, was broken. She knew that she was obliquely punishing him, and that it was unfair, but she couldn't help herself. Her coldness was not feigned; she felt that emotion had died in her, although there was still a deep, inescapable ache in her heart for what might have been if only Jordan had loved her enough. . . .

Because he never had loved her deeply and strongly,

she was convinced of that. He had been sorry for her, fond of her and undoubtedly sexually attracted to her. But that wasn't love. He was passionate and he was possessive, but that wasn't love. Instead of understanding her need to grow in her own way, he had tried to coerce her into some mould that he had devised for her—and that wasn't love. And that was what she couldn't forgive. He had made her love him and given so little of himself in return.

He grew short-tempered and irritable, ceased touching her altogether, and his face assumed a habitual wary blankness instead of the tight-mouthed control that had earlier followed the turning of her cheek, her slight but definite physical recoil, when he had attempted to caress her.

Strangely, she found that she missed the fleeting warmth of his lips on her cheek or temple, the brushing of his fingers on her arm, the hard strength of his hand cupping her shoulder.

And then there came an evening when they attended a party together and she looked up from a discourse that an earnest young man was pouring into her ear, something about the Canadian economy, and saw Jordan laughing with a young woman who had her hand on his sleeve and her lifted, smiling face close to his shoulder.

She felt a most extraordinary emotion take hold of her, a mixture of sheer pleasure in the picture he made with his dark head thrown back a little and his eyes glowing with humour, and a tearing pain because it was so long since he had laughed like that with *her*. The girl leaned towards him as he lowered his head, so that their faces were close as she said something else to him, something that brought a different gleam to his eyes and a look that Keely remembered to his face—a look that had not been directed at her for months. And she found her hands clenching tightly in her lap and a swift rush of anger warming her cheeks.

As he drove home through the darkened streets she asked him who the girl was, and he said she was the daughter of an old acquaintance. 'I used to take her about a bit at one stage,' he added casually. 'Jenny was always good fun.' He smiled reminiscently, and she looked away, wondering viciously what sort of *fun* he was thinking of. 'Intelligent, too,' he mused. 'She's a television producer now. And very good, I believe.'

'She isn't married?'

'No. She prefers the single life, it seems.'

'Wise girl.' She glanced sideways, and in the light from the street lamps saw the tightening of his jaw. He drove the rest of the way in stony silence.

She met Jenny again, and Melina and Dorothy and Lisa—it seemed to Keely's heated imagination that whenever they went out, or entertained, there was a succession of lovely girls who flirted and laughed with her husband, who could bring to his eyes an appreciative gleam and to his lips a smile that never appeared in his wife's company. Keely seethed in silence, presenting a cold, calm facade with no more than a small, uncaring social smile on her face, but one evening, after their guests had departed and Jordan had actually run the dark, petite Melina home to her apartment, she made the mistake of waiting for him.

She pretended to be clearing away glasses and emptying ashtrays, and when he came in she didn't look up, continuing with her task as though he weren't there.

'Leave it,' he said. 'Surely we pay that woman for that sort of thing.'

'She'll do the washing up,' Keely said quietly. 'I don't like leaving a mess of glasses about; it's depressing. And the ashes make the room smell.' She hadn't meant to say any more, but her voice went on. 'You're back very quickly.'

'It wasn't far.'

'Didn't Melina ask you in for a nightcap?'

'Actually, yes,' he said deliberately.

She straightened suddenly, anger shooting through her, and she caught the quick flash of satisfaction in his eyes before she looked away. She put the glasses she was holding onto a tray and said, quite coolly, 'I'm surprised you didn't accept.'

'Why?' His voice sounded abrupt and hard.

'You seem to enjoy her company.'

He paused before answering, and his voice was studiedly casual. 'Why not? It's very pleasant company.'

Keely's mouth compressed. She picked up the tray and made to pass him with it, but he stood in front of the door and didn't move.

'Excuse me,' she said frigidly.

'Why are you angry, Keely?' he said, a gleam in his grey eyes.

'I'm not angry!' she snapped. 'I just want to get these into the kitchen.'

He took the tray from her, jerking it from her hands so that the glasses rattled together, and put it down on a side table. 'Leave it,' he said sharply. 'This discussion is just getting interesting.'

'To you, maybe. *I* don't find your lady friends all that fascinating!'

He laughed. 'Lady friends?' He grinned at her, and she felt that now familiar pain twisting in her heart. 'Yes, I suppose that's a fair description,' he said. 'You're not jealous, are you—because I enjoy a bit of pleasant female company now and then?' He paused then, eyeing her flushed face and tight lips with unsmiling eyes. 'There has been a lack of that commodity around here lately, hasn't there?'

'If you don't enjoy my company,' she said stiffly, 'it's a pity you ever married me, isn't it?'

'You know I didn't mean it like that!' he said, putting out his hand to her.

She shied away from his touch. As always, that angered him, and his expression hardened. 'You could hardly blame me,' he said, 'if I took more than companionship from some of my *lady friends.*'

'Well, why haven't you?' she asked waspishly. 'I'm sure they'd be only too willing!'

She saw the arrested expression in his eyes and flushed vividly.

'Dog in the manger, Keely?' he said softly. And then he smiled.

She thought he was going to move towards her, and she instinctively stepped back, anger and humiliation welling up inside her. Her hand brushed against one of the empty glasses on the table, and as she took in the pleased amusement in Jordan's smile, her hand closed round the glass and she threw it at his head.

She saw his face go stark with shock before he jerked aside, and the glass smashed noisily but harmlessly against the frame of the door.

She was shocked, herself, at what she had done and stood stiffly immobile as he slowly straightened and came towards her. 'Well, well!' he said as his eyes held hers unwaveringly. 'I thought you'd lost your capacity for emotion.'

So had she, but she was racked with emotion now, shaking with it. Jealousy and anger and a piercing hurt because he was enjoying this, looking down at her flushed, furious face with cruel laughter in his eyes.

She made a fierce effort at control and managed to stop trembling, clenching her fists by her sides and closing her teeth tightly.

Jordan said, 'Now, don't close up again, you little clam. You were doing rather well a minute ago.' His hands descended to her shoulders and held her strongly, as though he expected her to resist him.

She didn't, though her eyes went wary and her nerves tightened under his touch. 'Let me go,' she said, barely moving her lips.

'Oh, no!' he said calmly. 'I'm going to find out if you're capable of another kind of emotion after all.'

She said, 'No!' and made a frantic, shortlived effort
at escape, but his mouth stopped her protest and his
hands easily dealt with her struggles. In the end she
gave up fighting and stood rigidly resistant, but unmoving, in his arms.

His kiss bruised, and at first she felt a stirring of
triumph because her initial reaction was mainly stinging
contempt that he thought her so easily conquered. But
as he kissed her again and again, his mouth moving
firmly and warmly over hers, her head tipped back over
his encircling arm, a faint tremor of desire began to
kindle deep inside her.

Alarmed by it, she made a convulsive movement of
denial, quickly stilled as his hands tightened their hold
on her. He shifted his feet, bracing his legs apart to
thrust his body intimately against hers, and as she tried
to voice a protest against his invading mouth he took
advantage of the involuntary parting of her lips to kiss
her more deeply and thoroughly. The objection she was
trying to voice died in a sighing breath that was lost in
his kiss.

He gave her no respite, and the spiralling of desire
became insistent and urgent until it no longer mattered
that he had hurt her and not loved her enough. She had
forgotten altogether about Melina and Jenny and all the
others. She knew only that it was too long since Jordan
had made love to her like this, that she loved him
desperately and that her body needed the ultimate
closeness and loving of his.

Her resistance when he moved her back into the
room and thrust her down on the sofa was only a token
thing, a reflex action that he didn't take seriously at all.
He took the hands she pushed against him and pinned
them beside her head, his eyes brilliant with impatient
passion, and said, 'Stop it, you little fool! You want it as
much as I do.'

Her sharp, shuddering sigh as his mouth found the
softness of her breast confirmed it, and she arched her

body against him and surrendered at last, her hands, as
he released them, clutching and caressing his shoulders.

It was the end of the long drought, and there was no
question after that night of pretending an indifference
to him physically. She knew that Jordan was satisfied
that there was no further problem, and she told herself
that their marriage was saved and that she was happy.
She tried to suppress a quite illogical resentment that
sometimes made her want to hurt him, to prick him
with barbed remarks. But as she noticed that his
interest in other woman did not seem to have waned,
the pinpricks became more frequent; she hated herself
for doing it, but watching him look with lazy masculine
admiration at another woman obscurely wounded her,
and her pride demanded its small revenge.

Jordan didn't seem to care. He laughed at her and
verbally slapped her down, his capacity for hurt far
greater than hers, although she would have died rather
than let him know it. And he still made love to her,
knowingly and with an insight into her most secret
needs, which brought her to almost unbearable heights
and made her nearly hate him afterwards.

It was at this time that Peter Gainham came back
into her life.

Peter had remained with her father's firm after the
takeover and had been transferred to Canada and
promoted by the company. It was inevitable that he
would seek Keely out. Perhpas it was inevitable, too,
that Peter would repeat to her his belief that Jordan had
had an eye to the main chance when he had married
her, and that in her present mood she was more
inclined to listen to such insinuations.

He was the only person in Canada who had known
her before her marriage, and when he told her that he
had been offered a still better salary and prospects back
in New York and would be returning there, her dismay
was disproportionate. She was not so very fond of

Peter, but he had come to represent a time when she
had been free and happy and cared for, with none of
the complexities, heartbreaks or unwilling dependen-
cies that her marriage to Jordan had brought her.

She must have betrayed more than she had realised
of her feelings. Peter said, 'Why don't you leave him,
Keely?' And when she looked at him in stunned shock,
he urgently took her hands in his and said, 'You're not
happy with him, are you? I can see it in your eyes. They
never used to look so . . . haunted.'

With an effort, she laughed and denied it and told
him he was imagining things. But that week, Jordan
went to Toronto on business—or so he told her. And
one night when she was watching television, he suddenly appeared on the screen. It was a fleeting close-
up, and the camera almost immediately panned back
to show that he was one member of an audience—an
audience gathered to honour a famous, venerable TV
star who had reached his eightieth birthday. But the
man Keely had seen had certainly been Jordan. And
the woman sitting beside him, her hand on his lapel as
she smilingly turned to speak to him, her lips almost
touching his cheek, was definitely Jenny Warren, the
girl he had told her was intelligent as well as beautiful,
whom he had once 'taken about' and who was, Keely
recalled all too vividly, 'always good fun.'

At first she felt numbed, and then angry. And then
the seed which Peter had planted all at once took root
and grew with monstrous rapidity. When Jordan returned at the end of the week, he found a note saying
that she felt their marriage had been a mistake, that
they would both be happier apart and that he could, if
necessary, contact her through the legal firm that had
previously dealt with her father's affairs.

Chapter Ten

Keely's thoughts were returned to the present by a distant crash, followed by a profound silence and then a chorus of childish giggles.

Curious, she followed the sounds to the kitchen and found Tila there with about a dozen little girls. Two of them were inexpertly sweeping up the fragments of a large earthenware bowl which had evidently fallen to the stone floor, and Tila, with a resigned expression but a twinkle in her eye, was directing several others while they mixed something in another bowl, their brown arms whitened with flour to the elbows.

Tila looked up as Keely came into the room, and said, 'Oh, did the noise frighten you, Keely? These clumsy girls dropped their bowl.' For some reason, the girls began to giggle again at this, and Tila clapped her hands and said something sternly in Fijian. Turning to Keely again, she said, 'I help the teacher at the village school by taking a group of girls for a domestic science lesson each week. But my discipline is not so good, I think.'

Keely looked at the little girls, who were busily applying themselves to their tasks but taking rapid little peeps at her from dark, mischievous eyes. 'What about the boys?' she asked.

'Oh, they are taught carpentry by one of the village carpenters,' Tila said.

Of course, Keely thought, and said, 'I won't disturb you. Good luck with the lesson.'

She left the kitchen and went towards the stairs, thinking how cut and dried everything was here— cooking for the girls and carpentry for the boys, husbands working at the phosphate plant and the plantation, wives looking after the children and making the tapa cloth, doing the washing and feeding their families. As she reached the stairs Jordan came in the door, for a moment catching her eyes with his. This place would suit him, she thought, and without speaking turned away from him and began to go up to her room.

She heard his swift footsteps behind her, and then a hand grasped her arm and turned her to face him.

'What was that in aid of?' he asked.

'What?'

'That look you just gave me,' he said.

He must have seen something in her face, she supposed. She shook her head and shrugged. 'I was just thinking how you must love it here,' she said.

He frowned. 'In what way?'

'You've always believed a woman's place is in the home, haven't you? Well, there's certainly no confusion of roles in this place. Division of labour, right down the line. I bet Salutuan men never wash a single dish.'

He grinned, a little sardonically. 'No, they don't. Tila and Kanimea were adamant that I had to have a woman to do the housework—otherwise the islanders would never take me seriously.'

'Lucky you. Six months here must have reinforced all your—'

'Prejudices? I'm not the only one with those, Keely.'
He released her arm and began to walk beside her as
she turned to ascend the stairs. 'People change,' he
added. 'And, as a matter of fact, I never did believe
that all women should be confined to the home. I
number some very talented women among my staff—
and my friends.'

'Yes,' she said, with bitter remembrance. 'But your
wife mustn't be one of them, must she?'

'It wasn't quite as simple as that.'

They had reached the door of her room, and she put
her hand on the knob and said, 'Wasn't it? I got the
message loud and clear at the time.'

She opened the door and he pushed it wider and
came into the room with her. 'I told you to do what you
wanted,' he said. 'I didn't stop you . . . pursuing your
career.'

'You grudged every minute I spent on it,' she said.
'And you punished me for it.'

'Punished?'

'*Yes!*'

She saw him concentrating, frowning, as he thought
back. Then he said slowly, 'Is that what you thought
then?'

'What else?' she asked bitterly.

And with a bitterness to match her own, he said, 'My
God, woman—did it never occur to you that I was
hurt?'

'Hurt?' she whispered in stunned surprise, and his
mouth twisted as he said, 'No, I don't suppose it did.'

Then he turned and left her, closing the door behind
him with a gentle click.

At lunch, she looked at him with new curiosity, but
his face gave nothing away. She was startled when he
suddenly looked up and found her watching him. He
said, out of the blue, 'Is Peter Gainham waiting for you
back home?'

'What?' She was quite bewildered. 'Of course not!'
she said emphatically.

He raised his eyebrows. 'You're not with him anymore?'

Anger began to replace her surprise. 'I never was *with* him!' she said loudly. '*Never!* You had no reason to think so.'

'You left with him. . . .'

'*What?*'

She saw the sudden doubt in his eyes as he said, 'You left when he did—and I'm not blind, Keely. The two of you had been living in each other's pockets ever since he arrived in Vancouver.'

'And on *that* evidence, you assumed—'

'There was more. Peter told someone he had asked you to go away with him.' A fleeting expression of distaste crossed Jordan's face. 'Someone who felt he should mention it, when I got back from Toronto and found you had left me.'

'He didn't exactly ask me that!' she protested. 'And I wouldn't have, anyway. I've never cared for Peter in that way.' The mention of Toronto had touched on a raw spot, and she said, 'And even if I had, *you're* hardly in a position to throw stones.'

He frowned and pushed his chair back a little. 'What do you mean by that?' he demanded.

'You were with Jenny Warren in Toronto,' she said baldly.

'Yes,' he said instantly. 'For a short while. How did you know?'

'I saw you,' she told him. 'On TV.'

He looked at the accusation in her eyes and said, 'Well, that's hardly *in flagrante delicto*. You do mean that you thought I was having an affair with Jenny, I presume?'

'What else?' she said, infuriated by his calm manner.

The calmness vanished. He pushed his chair completely away and stood up. 'What else?' he repeated. 'I happened to have been staying in the same hotel as Jenny—if you'd known *that* it would have been grist for your busy little mind, wouldn't it? But as a matter of fact it was pure coincidence. She had no escort for the evening, since the man who should have taken her had gone down with some kind of bug, and she didn't want to go alone. I filled the gap. And if you had been there when I got home, no doubt I would have told you all about it. You're not going to tell me *that* was why you left me?'

'No,' she said. That had been the catalyst, but not the real reason.

Jordan said, 'But you didn't leave me for Peter Gainham?'

'How could you think so?' she asked in a low voice.

'It wasn't that hard,' he said. 'I hadn't been able to make you happy. I thought that perhaps he could.'

Keely shook her head.

Jordan said, 'If not Peter—someone else? Is there anyone else, Keely?'

He looked at her penetratingly, and she thought, fleetingly, of the man in New York who was waiting for her to come back and give him an answer, and she knew now that the answer must be no. 'There is someone,' she said slowly. 'He wants to marry me.' He was a nice man, and gentle, and he loved her. And she had thought that if she could see Jordan once more and put him out of her heart for good, she could obtain a divorce and be contented with a good, safe, affectionate man.

Jordan said, 'Are you going to marry him?'

'I'm still married to you,' she said. 'Would you give me a divorce?'

'Is that why you really came here?' he asked harshly. 'To ask me to free you?'

She could have done that through their lawyers. The truth was much more complex. 'I came hoping to free myself,' she said.

His hands were thrust into his pockets and his face looked taut, a dark flush on the cheekbones, but there was a whiteness about his sternly held mouth. 'You can have your divorce,' he said. 'But there's a condition.'

'Condition?' she looked at him almost dazedly. *Why* was he offering her a divorce? For her sake, or because he wanted his own freedom?

'We never did have a honeymoon, did we?' Jordan was saying. 'But what better place for a belated honeymoon than a tiny Pacific island? I don't see why a marriage can't end as it should have begun.'

'What are you suggesting?'

'It isn't a suggestion,' Jordan said silkily. 'It's a condition. You spend the next few weeks with me, *as my wife,* and you can have your divorce.'

Her mind churning with a conflict of emotions, Keely said weakly, 'That's an *insane* idea!'

Jordan said carelessly, 'Humour me!'

'You can't be serious!'

'I *am* serious.'

She looked at him and saw that he was. A disjointed series of fears, hopes and wild guesses at his motives flitted through her brain. Then she said slowly, 'All right. I accept your . . . conditon.'

It was like going back in time—and yet different, for this was a time that never had been. When they had first been married, there had been no long days idling together in the sunshine after swimming in warm tropical waters; no leisurely walks, with no particular object in view, along miles of crisp white sand or through dark, shadowing palms and breadfruit trees; no exploration of the mysteries of a coral reef, swimming among shoals of brilliantly coloured fish, finding gracefully waving fronds of strange, exotic seaweeds and causing vivid anemones to close at the touch of their fingers. And no secret, magical cave like the one Jordan guided her to by diving underwater to the entrance, coming up in a grotto where the translucent blue water cast moving flashes of light on the white walls and high ceiling and lapped against a crescent of pure, unmarked sand at the other end of the cave.

In the dimness, they stood on the sand together, dripping from their swim, the only sounds the lapping of the water against the sides of the small space and their own breathing. Jordan put his hand on her damp waist and drew her closer as she shivered.

'Cold?' he asked her, his lips brushing her temple.

'Not really. It's sort of—eerie, isn't it?'

'There are supposed to be ghosts here.'

'I'm not surprised. What ghosts?'

'A pair of lovers. They were hiding in here from the girl's father, who wanted to kill the young man for seducing his daughter, and a hurricane came up, raising the water level in the cave until they drowned.'

Keely shivered again, and Jordan pulled her hard against him. 'They died happy,' he said, 'wrapped in each other's arms, and when the wind rises one can hear their sighs of passion—'

At that moment, a long, breathy, sound seemed to echo about the cave and Keely stiffened, giving a startled exclamation.

Jordan laughed softly, and said, 'There it is! Actually, the air in the cave comes through a narrow opening, and the wind rushing down it quite often makes that sound.'

'Heavens!' Keely relaxed, and laughed a little, too. His arms tightened, and as she tilted back her head, his lips slid down the skin of her throat and back again to claim her mouth. She swayed against him, their wet bodies clinging together in a mutual flaring of desire, and Keely thought with sudden clarity that she would be happy if she died now, like this, in Jordan's arms.

The sigh came again, and Jordan reluctantly released her and said, 'The wind must be coming up. We'd better get out of here.'

They swam back to the canoe moored outside the cave and made for the beach below the big house. The wind was whipping the leaves of the palm trees about, and a faint clacking sound came from the stiff fronds as

they were thrown against one another. The sea outside
the reef was liberally sprinkled with whitecaps, and
even the waves rolling to the beach were higher and
choppier than usual.

'Looks like we're in for a storm,' Jordan said,
hurrying her towards the house. Huge black clouds
seemed to pursue them as they struggled up the path
with the wind pushing them first one way and then the
other. As they neared the white portico, large droplets
of rain began splashing down.

They ran up the steps hand in hand, laughing, and
Jordan slammed the big door closed behind them. 'I'd
better check the shutters,' he said. 'This could be quite
a wind.'

She left him to do it and went upstairs to change. She
had augmented her meagre wardrobe with some extra
sulus bought at the company store in the village, and
she put on a green and brown patterned one with her
white blouse, brushed her hair thoroughly and then sat
with her chin in her hands, gazing absently into the
mirror without seeing her own reflection.

Already she had been on the island for three weeks,
and this strange honeymoon must end when the ship
came back next week. She was still not sure what
Jordan had hoped to gain from it. Perhaps he had
merely been determined to make the most of the
convenient fact of her being here. He had, he said,
been without an intimate relationship for two years.
Perhaps that had been reason enough. A cold-blooded
reason, and one she would have believed without
hesitation when she first arrived. But during these last
few weeks she had, in a sense, come to know her
husband more intimately than in the two years she had
lived with him. Perhaps the fact that she was older had
given her a greater insight into his character. And there
was the fact that, by tacit consent, they had avoided
speaking of their previous relationship, which had led
to discussions of their earlier years, and on Jordan's

part to a fuller description of his relationship with his
grandparents than he had ever volunteered before.

'This is the first time,' he had told her, 'that I've been
really away from my grandfather—because after his
death, the company became a symbol of him. I never
realised before what a profound influence the old man
had on me. He loved me, I know—but he loved his
company more, really. All else was a means to an
end—the good of the company. I worshipped him as a
child, and even though I went through the usual
teenage rebellions, I never really saw the old man's
faults, only his virtues.'

'What were his faults?' Keely asked softly.

'The main one was putting his business before his
personal relationships,' Jordan said. 'I think, after my
grandmother died, that he regretted that. But at the
time, I didn't realise it. I went on following in his
footsteps until—'

'Until—?'

'Until I met you,' he said bluntly. 'And bought a
business that was going bankrupt, because—'

He stopped abruptly, and Keely said, *'What?'*

'Nothing. Forget it.'

But although he wouldn't say any more, Keely
couldn't forget it. She could fill in the details for
herself. She wasn't stupid. Jordan hadn't made a sharp
deal at all when he had bought out the business after
her father's death. Peter had been quite wrong. She
recalled now some puzzling remarks one of the direc-
tors had made, when she had been too grief-stricken to
take much notice. Something about it being fortunate
that Mr. Lang had 'changed his mind,' and how relieved her father would have been if he had known.

He hadn't been going to buy at all, but had decided
to do it after her father's death. And apparently it had
been no bargain. No wonder he had asked her if she
had any qualifications. If her father was almost bankrupt there would have been no money left for her. And

the money that Jordan had banked in her name, allowing her to believe it was the proceeds of the sale, must have come from his own pocket.

And he had married her—why? Had it been out of pity?

He had told her only yesterday, she recalled, as she stood on the beach towelling her hair dry, that she had changed. 'You're a woman,' he said. 'You stand on your own now, don't you?'

And she said, 'Yes.' She had had to get away from him to do that.

He looked at her enigmatically, and she wondered if he was glad, glad that she had grown independent, that she didn't need him and that he wasn't responsible for her.

'Have *you* changed?' she asked him, standing with the wet towel in her hands.

'Yes. Doesn't it show?'

'I'm not sure. At first I thought that you had grown even harder. But now I'm not sure if the changes are in you or in my knowledge of you. I was very young before, Jordan.'

'And I was very much the old man's grandson,' he said. 'Since coming here, I've been made to realise that people must be allowed to choose their own destinies. My grandfather's methods don't work on Salutu.'

'They don't work in marriage, either,' she said, quietly.

And Jordan said, 'They did for him.'

'But not for—everyone.'

'No, not for everyone.'

Sitting before the mirror, Keely pressed a hand over her eyes and leaned on it. If he realised now that he couldn't model his own marriage on his grandparents' pattern, was there hope for the future? But he had said he would divorce her. . . . Was that what he wanted? And if she told him that she didn't want a divorce after all, would he take her back out of pity, as he had possibly—very possibly—married her out of pity?

He came into the room then, and said, 'There's a hurricane warning out. I'm going down to the village to let the people know they can shelter here. Those *bures* won't stand up to it.'

'I want to come with you,' she said.

'Don't be silly—it's already wild out there.'

'I know. I want to photograph it.'

She looked him straight in the eyes and held her breath. He was standing with his head thrown back a little, his eyes narrowed but unreadable. There was a long, tense silence. Then he said, 'Okay. Get your camera.'

He made her change into jeans and a jersey, clothes she had not worn since being here, and then they braved the wind.

The trees seemed to be in a frenzy, and the beach was unrecognisable. Huge waves crashed over the reef and raced to the shore, and sand stung at her face as she closed her eyes against it. She staggered in the wind, and only Jordan's arm stopped her from being flung against a palm tree. She snapped a couple of quick pictures before they reached the village, which was in a flurry of activity as people tied things down, wrapped things up and gathered their families together.

In half an hour the village was evacuated, and Keely, who had climbed up a rise behind the place to take shots of the deserted huts and the furious sea in the background, was called down by an impatient Jordan.

She realised that everyone else had disappeared down the path into the trees, and she lowered the camera and began to run down the slope to join him.

Suddenly her ankle turned on a hidden stone among the grass, and, with a wrenching pain, she fell and rolled a few feet downhill.

When Jordan reached her she was sitting up, checking her camera anxiously for damage. He thrust it aside, and said, 'Never mind that thing! Are you all right?'

'I've twisted my ankle,' she said. 'Let me rest it for a few moments.'

But that didn't help, and when he pulled her to her feet and she tried her weight on it, the pain was so great that she cried out and felt dizzy.

'I'll have to carry you,' Jordan said. He retrieved the camera and swung her into his arms. Keely bit her lip hard to stop another cry of pain, and he said, 'Does that hurt, too?'

She shook her head, but her white face and tightened lips spoke for her, and he said, 'Liar. There'll be bandages at the company store. I'll bind it for you before we go any further.'

She managed to stand it until they reached the big corrugated iron building, and then Jodan placed her in a chair and searched the shelves until he found a roll of elastic bandage. He went out to the back and found some cold water and made a compress, and then he wound the bandage firmly about her now swelling ankle. The finished result was comforting, but the operation had made her feel faint again, and Jordan made her put her head down between her knees and went off once more to forage among the goods crammed on the shelves.

When he came back he had a white china cup in his hand, half filled with a pale liquid. 'Whisky,' he said. 'I can't find any brandy, I'm afraid.'

Keely grimaced. She wasn't a whisky drinker, but she bravely downed the fiery fluid and did feel braced by it. 'I'm all right now,' she said and, ignoring his sceptical look, stood up.

He caught her as she swayed and swung her into his arms again, but as he kicked open the door the full force of the hurricane struck the island. Keely heard a howling, furious note in the wind and saw leaves, whole branches and then, incredibly, an entire coconut palm, hurl themselves across the village compound. A *bure* shook, lifted and collapsed, then was caught up by the wind and carried away. Another was flattened by a tree which appeared from nowhere, and sheets of corrugated iron spun like scraps of paper as they were torn from roofs and flung away into the distance.

Jordan put her down and fought the door shut again. 'This is the most solid building in the village,' he said. 'We'll sit it out.'

The next few hours were a nightmare. Conversation was impossible because of the noise as the wind screamed on and because the roof and walls were battered by debris in a constant rain of sound. Then there was an indescribable rending, screeching, thunder of sound, and the roof of the store lifted above them and disappeared. Keely screamed and buried her face in Jordan's shoulder, and they huddled together in a corner near the counter while merchandise was torn from the shelves and rain pelted viciously down.

She heard Jordan's deep voice murmuring in her ear, saying words she wanted to hear but was afraid to believe, and knew that she was whispering to him, not knowing if he could hear her in the din, but wanting to tell him, because they were in danger and perhaps there would never be another chance, that nothing mattered in her life but him.

And at last it was all over. The wind died, and the rain disappeared, and the villagers, terribly anxious for them, arrived back and surveyed the wreckage of their homes. It touched Keely tremendously that Jordan's and her safety seemed to compensate them for the destruction all around.

Jordan fetched the Landrover and took her home by road, and as he laid her down on her bed, taking care of her injured foot, she said, 'What will they do? All their homes are gone.'

'They'll rebuild,' he said. 'But I think the copra will have had it. Perhaps now the council will consider a suggestion I made to them.'

'What's that?'

'I wanted to turn this place over to them to be run as

a hotel. If it was successful it would be an assured income, and if the crops failed they wouldn't be entirely without resources. It could tide them over.'

'It sounds like a good idea. I can imagine Tila running a hotel—she'd make it a success, I'm sure.'

An odd silence fell, and Jordan moved over to the window and opened the shutters. 'You can see the tears of morning now,' he said. 'Half of the trees have gone.'

The silence returned, and he said, 'When you asked me to let you come and photograph the storm—it was a test, wasn't it?'

'I suppose so,' she admitted.'

'Did I pass?'

'Yes. You wouldn't have let me two years ago, would you?'

'No.' He was half turned away from her, apparently still watching the waterfall in the distance. 'When Sven comes back—you'll be moving on.'

She had the feeling that he had just managed to stop that from sounding like a question.

'I have a commission to finish,' she reminded him.

He put up a hand to grasp the frame of the window, an oddly groping hand, and she took a breath and said, 'May I come back afterwards?'

'What for?' he asked almost wearily. 'To show me again how successful and independent you are?'

Again? Keely passed a tongue over dry lips, thinking back, beginning to realise what kind of defences he had put up when she had arrived here, and why. She had come here, been 'introduced' to him as *Miss* Alexander, and she had kept insisting that her only motive was to do a job. Of course, the job was genuine, and her editor was convinced it was all his own idea, but Keely had planted it in his head after a hurried, heart-in-mouth trip to Vancouver when she had heard a rumour that Jordan Lang had died. That had jolted her, showed her that she was still bound to him and had determined her to try and break the bondage. But she hadn't come to show off her success.

She said clearly, 'No. To show you how much I love you.'

For a horrible moment she thought he wasn't going to respond. He stood like a statue cast in bronze, unmoving and apparently unmoved.

Then he turned and she saw the blaze in his eyes, the movement towards her that he quickly checked. 'You *meant* what you said—down there?' he asked.

Surely anyone meant what they said in the teeth of a hurricane, Keely fleetingly thought. 'Didn't *you?*' she countered.

'*Yes!* But you've always known that I loved you.'

'Oh, Jordan!' Keely whispered unsteadily. 'I haven't!'

His face assumed a strangely rigid look. 'It may not have seemed much like love,' he admitted, with difficulty. 'I was selfish and possessive, I know. Try to understand, Keely, I was terrified of losing you.'

'Terrified?' she repeated. Jordan had always been so sure of himself, so aggressively certain of his power, that this revelation of insecurity shook her.

He came over and sat on the bed, taking her hands in a crushing grip. 'I'm not used to explaining my motives,' he said roughly, and she realised with inward astonishment that he was embarrassed. 'But I've had a lot of time to think since coming to Salutu. In some ways, it's the first time I've ever been able to completely escape the influence of my grandfather and the company.'

He paused, frowning, and Keely said, 'I always felt that the company was a kind of extension of "the old man," that all your love and loyalty belonged to it.'

'Did you? Then perhaps you *will* understand. My grandfather was almost obsessed with his business, and he brought me up—quite deliberately—to regard it as the most important thing in life. And also with a tremendous sense of the responsibility I owed to his memory. He instilled in me the fact that when he had gone it was up to me to carry on in the way he had taught me. And I always knew that although he loved me, it wasn't primarily for myself—I was the future of his precious company. That's why, when I married you, I wanted you to make up for that. I hoped that you would love me so wholeheartedly that you would never need or want anyone—anything—else. And I started off with you so wrongly that I could never be sure of you—and that was hell!'

'What do you mean—wrongly?'

'Keely, I took shameless advantage of your inexperience, your vulnerability after your father's death and the remnants of what you admitted was a teen-age crush to get you to consent to marrying me. I rode roughshod over your doubts—that was the way I had always got what I wanted, just as my grandfather did. It was the only way I knew, and, in my arrogance, I thought you would learn to love me. And yet, unconsciously, I think I was aware that if you grew out of your dependence on me, I might lose you. That's why I panicked when you took an interest in anything else but me.'

'And you reacted like a hurt child,' she said softly.

His mouth twisted wryly. 'I guess so. In fairness, I had no reason to stop you exercising your talent for photography, but even though I recognised that, it didn't stop me feeling savage about it. It wasn't meant as a punishment, as you thought. I simply couldn't help myself.'

'But Jordan—*you* spent so much time at the office. What should I have done?'

'I know it's unfair and illogical,' he said. 'But I was afraid of your career taking priority over our marriage —and yet I didn't realise that I had allowed the company, *my* career, to do just that. I've often felt that the company owns me, rather than the other way round.'

'You sound resentful,' she said. 'I always thought that you loved it, just as your grandfather did.'

'I came to hate it after you left,' he said. 'It was only

a complicated machine. One can't love a machine. Can one?'

He was looking at her with an almost pleading light in his eyes, and she realised that he was reminding her that she had called *him* a machine, a man without normal feelings. . . .

'I didn't mean that!' she said swiftly.

'Yes, you did. You told me so the next day. But believe me, it isn't true. I may be selfish and overbearing and have a filthy temper, and I don't deserve you, but I love you. And though I find it hard to credit after the brutal way I've treated you, you just told me that you love *me*.'

His eyes questioned her, and she smiled into them. His hands on hers tightened, and he said huskily, 'Do you still want that divorce?'

'What divorce?' Keely asked innocently.

The glimmer of a relieved smile lit his eyes. 'The divorce I offered you in an uncharacteristic moment of altruism.'

She looked down at the strong hands holding hers. 'I don't think it was so uncharacteristic,' she said.

'It was. But I swear I'll never try to bully you again. I've learned that one loves with an open hand, not a closed fist.'

'Yes,' she said. 'It's been a hard lesson, hasn't it? I'm sorry I didn't understand before.'

'How could you? I didn't understand myself.'

'Perhaps I was too young, anyway. We've both changed, Jordan. But I never really stopped loving you. I knew as soon as I saw you that it was still there, more powerful than ever.'

'And fought it.'

'Yes. And fought it, very unsuccessfully.'

He smiled and said, 'Tell me again!'

'Egotist! I love you—I always have and I always will. Satisfied?'

'No. But I could be, very easily. How's your ankle?'

'I hardly feel it.' She tipped her head back, responding to the glow in his eyes, and met his kiss, falling back on the pillows and taking him with her. Her arms locked about his neck, and his lips moved softly on her skin. The house was quiet, deserted but for the two of them, and all about it water dripped with soft, hurrying sounds from the wind-battered trees. She heard the distant rush of the waterfall and imagined the struggling sun lighting on the steady flow of droplets falling into the pool. Then Jordan's mouth returned to coax hers into passion, and she responded with uninhibited delight, knowing at last that this time there would be no tears in her morning.

Silhouette Romance

IT'S YOUR OWN SPECIAL TIME

Contemporary romances for today's women.
Each month, six very special love stories will be yours
from SILHOUETTE. Look for them wherever books are sold
or order now from the coupon below.

$1.50 each

Introducing
First Love from
Silhouette Romances for
teenage girls
to build their dreams on.

They're wholesome, fulfilling, supportive novels about every young girl's dreams. Filled with the challenges, excitement—and responsibilities—of love's first blush, *First Love* paperbacks prepare young adults to stand at the threshold of maturity with confidence and composure.

Introduce your daughter, or some young friend to the *First Love* series by giving her a one-year subscription to these romantic originals, written by leading authors. She'll receive two NEW $1.75 romances each month, a total of 24 books a year. Send in your coupon now. **There's nothing quite as special as a First Love.**

Silhouette Romance

15-Day Free Trial Offer
6 Silhouette Romances

6 Silhouette Romances, free for 15 days! We'll send you 6 new Silhouette Romances to keep for 15 days, absolutely free! If you decide not to keep them, send them back to us. You pay nothing.

Free Home Delivery. But if you enjoy them as much as we think you will, keep them by paying the invoice enclosed with your free trial shipment. We'll pay all shipping and handling charges. You get the convenience of Home Delivery and we pay the postage and handling charge each month.

Don't miss a copy. The Silhouette Book Club is the way to make sure you'll be able to receive every new romance we publish before they're sold out. There is no minimum number of books to buy and you can cancel at any time.